The Last Days of Il Duce

by

Domenic Stansberry

THE PERMANENT PRESS
SAG HARBOR, NY 11963

Library of Congress Cataloging-in-Publication Data

Stansberry, Domenic.
    The Last Days of Il Duce/ by Domenic Stansberry
       p. cm.
    ISBN 1-57962-004-3
    I.. Title.
    PS3569.T33353L47   1998
    813'.54--dc21   97-21536
                                      CIP

First edition, February 1998

THE PERMANENT PRESS
4170 Noyac Road
Sag Harbor, NY 11963

The Last Days of Il Duce

ONE
A VISION IN THE FOG

My name is Niccolò Jones, and I'm writing this down in the prison yard at Coldwater Penitentiary. Three people I used to know are dead. Two of them I loved, the other I hated—though lately I am less sure about the difference between those feelings. I tell myself it doesn't matter. Either way, I do little else but imagine the day I'll be out of here.

I see myself walking those bleached white streets, under that startling sun, and I climb the long hills above North Beach. When I get to the top, I look down at the blue Pacific. Like in a dream I see the deep channels, where the cold water of the ocean mixes with the bay, and I think about all those tourists eating their lunches beneath the stone walls of Alcatraz. They are like flocks of birds, those tourists. When I was a kid, my mother took us to the old island prison on Fugazi's steamer, and I stood out on that rock, looking back at my neighborhood across the water. Maybe when I climb that hill and take my last look around, the wind will get into my eyes, and I'll feel like that kid again, longing for the blind alleys of home. But sooner or later I'll walk back down that hill, and I'll leave Chinatown and North Beach and all these streets forever.

When my brother and I were growing up in North Beach, they called us the Abruzzi boys. We would walk down the street together and watch the old men playing bocci in Columbus Gardens. The teenage punks would joke and laugh and yell out:

"Here comes the Abruzzi boys!" Then they would rough up our thick black hair with their long fingers.

In fact our name was not Abruzzi but Jones. Niccolò and Joseph Jones. My father was where the Jones came from. He was a carpenter, or had been before he went lame in the war. It was my mother who was the Abruzzi, and though we were only half Italian, that's what counted in this neighborhood. So we were the Abruzzi boys.

We came to the park to watch the old men roll the bocci

around, but more than that we came because the Catholic school girls would be there too, dressed in their pleated skirts and white blouses. Their eyes were big and brown and their hair was dark and their gestures seemed always about to reveal some secret. They were flirtatious in the way that girls in our neighborhood were, not with us but with each other and their grandfathers. In their more daring moments, though, they smiled sidelong at those angular boys a few years older than ourselves, who carried on their bodies a vague animal smell mixed with the grime and sweat of the city. There was one particular girl. Maybe her eyes were darker, her skin more olive than all the rest, or maybe it was the way her skirt fell across her knees. I don't like to think about her now, but back then my brother Joe and I would watch her thin brown legs from across the park, and later we would whisper her name to one another in the darkness of our bedroom on Vallejo Street.

Sometimes Micaeli Romano, the lawyer, would come and sit on the park bench beside us, and he would watch the girls too. Romano was in his early 40's then, a purebred Genovesi whose iron-black hair had recently started to gray. We knew him because some afternoons he drank beer with my mother at our kitchen table. One day at the park my little brother got up and left because he did not like Micaeli Romano. Micaeli patted my arm.

"Joe's a good boy," he said. "Your little brother loves his father. But you, you're a good kid too, Nick Abruzzi. You have your mother's brains. You'll make something of yourself, and I'll help you, when the time comes. Your mother has high hopes. For both of you."

He gave me a wink and I realized right then there was a part of me that hated Romano too; he was so sly and good-looking and everybody admired him so much. Though I was too young yet to know the stories that went through the neighborhood, I saw how he glanced at my mother when her back was turned, looking her up and down, and I saw too the small tight smile of pleasure on my mother's face. At that moment, I didn't care. Instead I was glad to be seen with him, the important man, the successful Italian, the big shot lawyer Micaeli Romano. People looked at us and I liked that. Because one of those who looked was the girl whose name my brother and I whispered in the dark. Marie Donnatelli. The girl of the brown hair and brown eyes. With whom one day my brother and I would laugh and tussle down at Ocean Beach, where the sky is always gray, and the three of us—Marie and myself and Joe—would roll over one another and tumble in the high dunes. But I'm getting off my story and I promised myself I would tell it straight.

It was 1986, almost thirty years later, on a Thursday night, and I was drinking in a Chinatown bar named Kim's. It had been called something else before, Salvadore's or Dante's or Marino's, I don't quite remember, there's been so many along here; then the old Italian who owned the place sold out. It used to be you could glance inside and see all the old Italians drinking their American beers. They would be staring across the bar at pictures of their relatives as they looked when they first came over from the old country: all mustachioed, wearing those baggy pants and fat suspenders. For some reason Kim's still had the pictures of those dead Italians on the wall, even though most of its clients now were Chinatown downbeats, old yellow men who spoke no English if they could help it and who stared quietly over their Miller beers into the gloom of those Italian eyes.

I liked to sit there with those old Chinamen. It was quiet inside Kim's and when someone did talk, it was in a language I didn't understand.

There were certain things I didn't want to understand anymore. I was just past forty, that age when you wake up in the morning and feel something thickening inside and only people too old to matter refer to you as a young man anymore. I had ruined my life in all the important ways, but I knew the small things that helped a man survive. For one, I nursed a beer pretty well. This night I nursed first one, then another, until finally it was Friday morning. I climbed off the stool and got out into the street without wobbling more than a little.

It was foggy outside and that fog was smothering everything. Kearny Street was empty and I could see down to Columbus, where some tourists fresh from the strip joints crossed the street. A woman in the group let loose a throaty laugh. Behind her a crumbum in rags rolled his shopping cart down the walkway. The woman glanced my way, I think, and the crumbum did too. The fog was warm and the muffling of sounds created an intimacy on the street between us. Then they all moved on and I was alone in Chinatown.

My soul was filled with an intimation of things to come, but I did not know what those things might be. I walked through a side alley heavy with the smell of pork grease and littered with vegetables from the Chinese stalls. I did not want to go home, so I went to the old Ching-Saw Hotel, where often there are young women in the lobby. Behind the desk was a jaundiced-looking white man, about my age, about my build, with the same kind of gut under his red polo shirt. Only my shirt was not red and his was embroidered with a Manchurian dragon over the pocket.

"All the girls are out. Convention in town."

"There's always a convention in town," I said and slid him the money anyway.

He gave me a hard once-over, then the pasty little grin that such men make their specialty. I gave him the grin back and sat in one of the lobby chairs to wait.

After a little while one of the girls returned, but she had a Chinese tourist with her—Portland, I guessed, from the moldy look of him—and they went upstairs together, pulling and tugging at one another's clothing. About the same time a group of Vietnamese street toughs wandered past the lobby window and into the side alley, disappearing behind the dumpster. I knew the routine here. The toughs were waiting for that tourist to come out the back door; then they would give him the business.

Maybe what the desk man had said about the convention was true. Because there was no in-and-out action in the lobby and I had to wait more than an hour, until at last a taxi pulled up and a girl stepped out alone. She was a small girl, whose hair was midnight black, and she looked at me wearily. It was getting on towards dawn.

Upstairs, she was more cheerful. We had a drink, and in bed she was still delicate but did not seem so small. She kept her eyes closed and her face was like a primitive mask, and she pushed herself against me, breathing heavily in my ear, while outside in the alley I could hear the Vietnamese boys joking around. After a while there was silence down in the alley, then the sound of the alley door creaking open. There was a thudding noise down there, over and over, a stifled cry, and a sound like a lead pipe against the concrete wall. All the while I still went after the Oriental girl. She lay beneath me, one hand under her head, her eyes still closed, and every once in a while grunting in a small fierce way. I knew she was tired, and suspected she was bored as well, but she went on moving her hips and my desire increased in a hopeless way until at last, her eyes still closed, she reached out and touched my face, and that small intimacy was all I needed. Outside there was a clattering in the alley.

"This your first time here?"

"Yes," I said. "I live alone. In a little cottage."

"In the city?"

"No. Out in the country. Down a shady lane."

I'm not sure why I lied. The truth was I lived two blocks over in North Beach. Maybe I wanted to her to think I was an innocent and then see how she treated me. I lingered a moment next to her, touching her as if I loved her—and maybe I did love her, just a little—then I stood up and put on my pants. The money I'd given the little man downstairs only covered the room fee, so I gave the girl what she wanted. At the last minute she reached up and pulled me by the shirt collar and whispered into my ear.

"Go out by the back door. Sometimes, the police, you know, they wait out front."

"Thanks, sweetie."

As I left the room I felt a small pang in that part of my heart that pretends to be innocent, but I still knew better than to listen to the girl. The back door was for the out-of-towners and fools, thinking they were sneaking away, discreet as hell, only to get mugged by the Viet punksters in the alley. Probably one of them was the whore's brother.

I walked out the lobby but in the end it wouldn't have mattered, not tonight. Because the kids had already scattered and the Chinese tourist, maybe fifty years old, sat propped against the alley wall. He wore a handsome suit, I saw that, and when I stepped closer I saw he wore a red tie about his neck and they had used that to choke him pretty bad. His businessman's paunch hung over his belly, and his belt was undone as if he had forgotten to zip up.

Maybe he was dead but it wasn't much of my business, and I figured there wasn't much the San Francisco cops would do anyway except blame whoever stumbled close. So I left him where he was.

It was almost dawn now and the pastry shops along Columbus were starting to open. I went into Antonio's, the owner of which I've known since I was a kid, but like a lot of the people in the neighborhood Antonio wouldn't talk to me since I'd gone to work for Jimmy Wong. He didn't mind selling me his coffee though, and I didn't mind sitting in his window and looking out toward Washington Square. The square was filling, as it did every morning, with Asian men and women doing Tai Chi, not just a dozen or even a hundred but a thousand or so, every shape and color and age, all of them stabbing at the air, huffing and saluting the rising sun, while meanwhile a few old wops sat on their green benches, in the middle of the park, reading *L'Italia* as if nothing in the world ever changed.

I was tired and decided to go home. The sun was breaking through earlier than usual, the blue sky showing over the cathedral spires, so for a minute the Asians seemed to be cast in great shadows of light. I paused to look at them and then across the park I saw someone else watching. My brother's wife. Or his ex-wife. Rumor said she was sleeping with Micaeli Romano's boy now. She dyed her hair these days, a snowy blonde, like some Italian women do, thinking to make themselves American, but I still knew it was her.

She turned then, Marie Donnatelli, and her eyes met mine from across the park. Or I thought they did, though in another minute she was gone, walking the other way. I told myself it was no coincidence, us seeing one another that morning; Marie would soon circle back into my life. I had told myself the same thing before but that didn't matter. I told it to myself again when I went home and lay down to fall asleep, envisioning once more that moment when I had looked across the park, the smell of the Asian girl still on my body, and seen Marie emerging from the fog.

TWO
AN EVICTION

In the morning I got a call from Jimmy Wong. A few weeks before he'd had me serve some papers on the Mussos, down on Filbert Street, and now Jimmy wanted me to go down with the Lee brothers to make sure the Mussos got out of his building on time.

The Mussos' apartment wasn't much but I could sympathize. My apartment wasn't much itself, just two rooms and a stove over the racket of Columbus Avenue, but I didn't want to get tossed out either.

"It's almost noon, Abruzzi. You hungover again?"

"No," I said. It was almost the truth. It takes a lot for me to get hungover. Still Wong could hear the netherworld in my voice and the clock said eleven-thirty. Four hours, I told myself, that's all the sleep I'd gotten. I remembered clutching my pillow and dreaming of the Chinamen dancing in the blue fog.

"Ed and Rickie will be out front of the Mussos' at one. You be there too and make sure things go smooth. No trouble."

"Since when do you have any trouble?"

"That's what I mean. That's why I want you there. You're a good lawyer, Abruzzi, if you didn't drink so much."

Wong said things like this but he knew the truth about me, or at least he had something close figured out. Otherwise I wouldn't be doing for him the work I did. It had been five years since I'd had an office bigger than the desk in my apartment, even longer since I'd done anything those in the profession might consider the practice of law. I hadn't been disbarred though, so I guess this counted for something.

"You come by when you're done. I got some more work for you."

There was no sense in sleeping now. I grabbed a grinder from a cart on the street and ate sitting on the grass in Washington Square. A couple of old wops gestured at me,

12

men of Romano's generation, and I could see them talking me over from their places on the bench. No doubt they were saying what a worthless son I was, disgrace of the neighborhood, the kind of thing old wop men are always saying. I lay back in the grass so I wouldn't have to see them, and I stared up at the spires of the Church of Saints Peter and Paul.

I didn't want to think about the old Italians. I wanted a drink but it was almost twelve-thirty now, and I didn't want to go evict the Mussos with liquor on my breath. It is easy for me to keep my mind empty when I sit in a darkened bar, raise a glass to my lips, then a cigarette, then open my sweet chops and watch the smoke come pouring thoughtlessly out. It's not so easy when you're lying out in the bright sun, staring up at the spirals of the cathedral where your brother married the woman you love and, years later, Father Campanelli whispered the liturgy over your mother's casket, your father sobbing in the pew for everyone to hear.

An old woman joined the old men on the bench. The three of them spoke in Italian, I figured, pointing every once in a while at me in the way one points at a child who does not yet have the ability of speech. It wasn't hard for me to guess the kind of things they were saying.

A mama's boy, that one. UCLA. Law School. Little Rose Abruzzi nearly died giving birth to him. Big shot office downtown, Mr. Lawyer, but look at him now. A bum in the park. That's what you get, you mix an Abruzzi and a Jones. But who listens to an old man these days? Who listens to anyone?

I did not want to have my life picked over like this. I decided to leave but before I could get myself away, the old ones were already up and stuttering over their canes. I peered into their ancient faces and thought I recognized Charlie Marinetti, a schoolteacher so many years ago, and though he gestured in my direction, and seemed to be looking where I stood, I realized he did not recognize me at all. Because as the old ones crept by I heard them talking. Not of me, but of Mussolini and Claratta Petacci. Arguing over which one of them it was who ruined Italy, or whether it was not Il Duce and his mistress at all but the Ligurians in general, or the Sicilians, or the hardheads from Calabria. Then they halted mid-stride, pointing back in my direction but still not seeing me, discussing some event that had happened long ago, maybe, here on this spot where I stood.

I went down to the Mussos on Filbert Street. They lived in an old wood frame building, set back in the alley, surrounded on all sides by a gravel walkway. This building, like the building next door and the fence that rose between them, had all been painted the same shipyard gray. The apartments inside the building were close on top of one another, and in the center ground between them was a cement yard, with a potted banana tree that received too much water and very little sun. These used to be cheap homes for the dockworkers but the docks were all closed now. It was all Chinese families except in the smallest apartments, where there lived the young clerks and aging bachelors of the financial district, who came home each night in their starched white shirts and lay alone in their beds thinking how someday they'd claw their way to a spot a little higher on the hill, maybe, where you could see over the concrete to the palm trees and the shimmering water.

The Lee brothers, Ed and Rickie, stood out front waiting for me, but the Mussos had themselves locked up tight inside their apartment. There was no pickup, no trailer, no U-haul truck, no sign anyone was getting ready to move.

Jimmy Wong liked to have someone like me around in situations such as this: someone the same skin and blood as the people being pushed out. There wasn't as much of this kind of business for me as there used to be, though we often found an old Italian or two, living in a rent-controlled apartment, whenever Jimmy acquired a new building.

Such was the case with the Mussos. They were still paying 1950's rent. We couldn't evict them for that, so I wrote up a damage complaint. When the Mussos went through the roof with the injustice of it and refused to pay, then I drew up the thirty-day notice and served it up, legal as hell, while Ed and Rickie Lee stood on the sidewalk with their arms crossed, just to emphasize the point. It was possible to fight us but that took money and brains, and people with both these commodities didn't do business with Jimmy Wong to begin with.

The Mussos' notice expired today. I knocked on their door. The lace curtains were drawn shut and it was quiet as death inside there, but I had been through this kind of thing before. Jimmy Wong had given me the key to the place. As soon as I stuck it in the lock, Mrs. Musso was all over me. She was about fifty, a small wiry-haired woman with plump breasts and beautiful, imploring eyes. She clasped her hands together, leaning against me, and dropped to her knees at my feet. Meantime her husband stood shame-faced in the middle of the living room, watching. All around us the apartment was filled with the kind of rococo junk that wops love.

"You can stay, if you just pay the bill. And sign a new lease, with the new rent."

My voice cracked a little as I spoke. Maybe because I knew it wasn't possible. Musso was an electrician, who made his living doing handyman jobs around the neighborhood, but he was getting old and no one hired guys like him anymore.

When he didn't answer, I motioned to the Lee brothers out on the street. They were thick-chested Chinese boys, stout like wrestlers, and they tripped a little as they came into the house. Mrs. Musso threw herself at me, her eyes wild and fierce. She pummeled me with both her fists and her body was up against mine too and all the while she yelled in Italian. I grabbed her by the wrists. I felt her breasts against me and felt too an embarrassing stir of desire, then she begin to sob and I let her go. I sat on the porch and lit a cigarette. The Lee brothers came out with a flowered lampshade, a chest of drawers, a ceramic pig from Italy. Then it was the couch draped in black lace, the picture of the Virgin, the stiff-backed chairs, the thirteen cans of olive oil. The stuff accumulated on the sidewalk. All this while I stared down into Chinatown, where the men in their gray suits and the women in their smocks and the little children with their black eyes all filled the streets, more and then more of them it seemed to me, while overhead the Chinese characters filled the signs, neon blinking in the

15

mid-afternoon, all those indecipherable letters rolling and tumbling into an upended martini glass over the liquor store.

After awhile the Mussos worked up some nerve. They came up next to me and Mr. Musso spit at my feet. "Curse you, Nick Abruzzi," he said.

"His name's not Abruzzi." Mrs. Musso looked at me in disgust. Her eyes were still beautiful. "He's a fucking Jones."

I'd had enough. I walked down to the Naked Moon to get a drink and watch the girls take off their clothes. While I was there I got on the phone to Wong and told him to send a truck over to the Mussos. I had an address for their kids down in the South Bay, and I was sure those kids had a swell place for all this stuff on the sidewalk, and also a couple extra rooms for Mom and Pop.

THREE
THE VALISE

Jimmy Wong's office was six flights up a building that didn't have an elevator. At least it didn't have an elevator the public could use. There was a coded one in the lobby, for office tenants and their employees, but for some reason Jimmy couldn't find it in himself to let me up that way. So it was the long climb up a dirty stairwell with a steel banister and concrete walls.

"You need the exercise," he said. "I walk those stairs every day."

Maybe it was true. Jimmy Wong was a fit-looking guy. He was about my age, and he had the smell of success on him and wore suits that were cut in Milan.

Wong had been born in San Francisco. So had his father and his father's father before that, but Jimmy had done better than any of them. He had a house over in Marin, and a pretty little wife who decorated the house, and a couple of kids in private school. His office was nothing fancy but it was on the top floor, overlooking the gaudy fronts and tin pagodas of Chinatown, so you could see all the way down to the Oakland bridge and the water beneath its girders. On his walls hung a picture of Chinese coolies building the railroads more than a hundred years ago, their backs all bent and faces weary. Jimmy had the habit of walking over and staring at that picture while you talked to him, then answering back, eyes empty, as if he hadn't heard a word. The truth was, he didn't give a fuck what you said, coolie or no. He made his money trading property, leveraging Hong Kong money into the neighborhood. He was pretty good at what he did, I guess, but I wouldn't want to have him for a landlord.

"I don't have your kind of stamina, Jimmy. You make all your clients climb those stairs? Or just the ones with weak hearts?"

Jimmy was studying his coolies. There was one white man in the picture, an overseer apparently, who seemed to be the only one aware of the photographer's presence. The overseer, who wore a battered derby hat, had one hand tucked in his waistband, as if posing; the other hand—through some flaw in the photograph, though it was hard to be sure—seemed to disappear into one of the coolie's skirts.

"I have something I need for you to deliver."

"Another notice?"

"No. A package."

It wasn't the kind of work Jimmy usually wanted from me. There was a leather valise on his desk, and he walked over and touched it with his fingers.

"I got a call yesterday. A friend of yours. Micaeli Romano."

"I didn't know you were acquainted."

"Our paths cross. Business matters. He asked if it was all right with me if he talked to you. He has some work for you. A job."

"He asked your permission?"

I acted surprised even though I knew it was the kind of thing Micaeli would do. Micaeli was very old-world, full of grace and decorum, the kind of man who did not shrink into himself with age. He seemed to respect others and so people respected him. Or most people did. He had done well as a lawyer, even served as a judge. His adopted son practiced real estate law and the two of them had some investments in that direction now, a holding company, properties scattered about the city.

"He asked me if it was all right he should talk to you. He wanted to be sure he wasn't stealing a valued employee."

"That's considerate."

My voice betrayed my resentment and I knew that resentment was something a man like Jimmy Wong—who respected his elders and his ancestors, especially the wealthy and powerful—could not understand. But Jimmy knew nothing of my life, how my feelings towards Micaeli Romano were all mixed up with my mother's admiration of him, my father's scorn, the meddling he'd done in our lives.

"He wants you to pay a visit."

"I'll think about it."

Jimmy held his hand tucked in his waistband. At length

he let go of what he was thinking and reached again for the valise. He took out a fat manila envelope that had been wrapped around with tape. Then a second envelope, similar but much thinner, as if there were only a paper or two inside. He examined them both a moment, then clasped them back up inside the valise.

"You deliver this to the address I give you. A man will answer the door and then you hand in the suitcase. He'll shut the door in your face but you stick around. In a minute, two minutes, who knows, he'll hand the case back to you. Empty. You bring the case back to me."

"Why don't I just take the envelopes?"

"It's nicer this way. I'll return the case to the client."

"It's not yours?"

"No."

I did not like the sound of this. I'd heard Jimmy Wong rummaged up and down the social ladder, at least for money, and there were other rumors too but I kept my ears closed to those kinds of things. So as far as I knew, Jimmy kept himself on the legal side of things, except for safety and fire code violations. (And some questionable evictions, too; though these last were my business, you might argue, and no one's sin but my own.) Still, Wong paid my retainer and if he wanted me to deliver the valise, then that's what I'd do.

"You don't have to worry, Jimmy. I'd kiss every whore in Chinatown for you."

I laughed but Jimmy did not think it was so funny. He was a family man. "It's not for me. It's a client delivery. From my point of view, it never happened." Then he handed me eight hundred dollars payment for delivering the package. I wondered how much had been Jimmy's cut.

"Come on, Jimmy. What's in the package?"

Jimmy Wong did not justify this with an answer. In his eyes was that sad expression I've seen before, when people wonder why it is I've thrown my life away. I reached over and touched the valise. Soft leather, very smooth, nice to the touch. As I examined it, Wong went on examining me, with more or less the same look, like that of a lamenting parent, a small gleam of hope in the eyes. I wondered if he

19

really saw me, or if for him it was not so much different than studying that ancient picture. I unclasped the valise and bounced the big envelope around in my hands. It felt like more cash in there, all bundled up. Then I took the other, thinner envelope, and ran it between my fingers.

"A love letter in here? A picture of the Golden Gate Bridge?"

Jimmy said nothing. Instead, his eyes were reproving, as if more concerned about my foolishness then the contents of the envelope. His eyes were suddenly ancient, regarding me as a child. It could be a drug deal, I guessed, or blackmail money. Or maybe just some peculiar Chinese business, documents from Hong Kong, paper lanterns, it didn't matter. I picked up the envelopes and stuffed them back into the case.

"All right. I could use the eight hundred."

Jimmy nodded. There was the barest trace of a smile. He walked me out to the elevator and punched in the code. He put one hand on his waist-band, and with the other hand he slid a piece of paper into my coat pocket. His cheeks glistened under the white light.

"This time, Mr. Jones, you go down in style," he said.

Inside the elevator I took out the piece of paper and read the address he had written there. It was a few blocks away, down Kai-Chin Alley. Nearby were the Friendship Housing Projects, a vast yellow building scrawled with Vietnamese graffiti. Street punks lounged on the doorsteps, sharp-looking youngsters who hunched their shoulders as they smoked and cast long looks down the alley. They acted as if they did not see you, as if a white man carrying a black leather case were invisible to their eyes, but I knew the people to whom you are invisible are the most dangerous of all. I had a friend who thought he was invisible like this during the fall of Saigon and ended up a sorry GI, drunk, pants down, disemboweled in Ho Chi Minh Alley.

I walked past the Viet punks, thinking maybe they were the same ones who'd asphyxiated the graying Chinaman the night before down at the Ching-Saw Hotel. When I looked back the Viets were gone and this bothered me more than if they had still been there. I felt like bolting but I was only half way down the alley. So I walked it slow, like a man who had business here, and found the number I was looking for. It was a dirty white door with a peephole in the middle. I knocked and waited. The alley smelled like piss.

I could feel my heart beating inside my head and I did not like the sensation. I glanced toward the safety of Kearny Street, where some young Midwestern girl was walking by with a camera. I knocked again, perhaps sooner then I should have, then the door burst open. The man who looked at me had the eyes of one to whom the whole world is invisible. His skin was paler than Wong's and the room behind him smelled of fish. His eyes were the eyes of a killer, I thought, and when he took the leather case those eyes looked me over, up and down, in a way that made me feel already as if I did not exist. Out in Kearny Street, the Midwestern girl was taking a picture of her boyfriend in front of the Buddhist temple. Some monks were beating drums on a balcony overhead and an old woman was crying. All these lives were going on, each one ignorant of everyone else, and none of us safe.

I returned the empty valise to Jimmy Wong, but it wasn't until I got inside Kim's Bar and drank my first beer that the feeling of impending danger began to fade, receding in the face of those Italian ancestors whose photos looked back at me from across the bar.

FOUR
JOE ABRUZZI, ON THE EVE OF HIS DEATH

My brother lived down in the Mission District now, with Luisa, his second wife. That Friday I met him, as I often did, at one of the old Irish bars on upper 24th Street; then we drove to Dolores Park. We stopped the car underneath a palm tree and passed the weed back and forth between us, like we've done ever since we were kids. I had pretty much given it up but my brother, even coming onto middle age, he still liked his dope.

From Dolores Park you can see over the high yellow palms to the pastel streets of the Lower Mission, which were all swamp and tule land before the Franciscans came and put the Indians to work. The Ohlone learned Christianity and then died with the anguish of the Franciscans in their hearts. Many of the Indians still lie buried beneath the park. The Mexicans in the neighborhood say you can see the souls of the Ohlone jolt loose, into the sky, each time we have a quake.

"It's still swamp down there," Joe said, nodding his head toward the barrio. "Don't let anybody fool you. It's a swamp and it's a slum. And I'm going to get the hell out."

Like my father, Joe was a carpenter, but unlike the old man he was restless by nature. He liked to be outside swaggering about under a blue sky, a hammer strapped to his belt. He always smelled of the sun, my brother, and of sawdust, and when he was a young son of a bitch, and strong, the girls would squat on the stoop across from ours and watch him unload his truck. One of those girls was Marie, though she never dated my brother until after I'd gone down to school, in southern California. By the time I came back she and Joe were a regular thing. I had taken up with a USC girl named Anne; she was pretty and smart and had parents who lived in a big house in Pacific Heights. The four of us double-dated. Marie was a wild one then, and I remember smelling the wildness of her as she draped herself around my brother in the front of the car and glanced battingly back at me and Anne. She wanted the car to go faster, she said;

she wanted—like an Aztec princess—to dip herself in gold; she wanted to touch herself and feel the thrill of her young body, like the thrill of reeds rustling in the high grass. Marie would say these things, or things close enough, and I would take Anne's hand and later, when we were alone, I would kiss Anne wildly about the lips. But in the end it was not Anne whom I loved and my brother could not hold on to Marie.

"I've got it figured," Joe said. "I've got a way out. I'm going to make a lot of money."

"How's Luisa?"

"Luisa's fine. Her kid's a crankster, a guy was knifed down the street, the house stinks of dry rot, but Luisa's fine. She whistles a happy tune."

Joe had married Luisa a couple years back, a Mexican woman with two kids of her own. Sometimes Joe could be pretty funny talking about their life together but he was a moody guy, who could swing from one emotion to the next without warning.

"I told you I'm putting together my own crew again, Nick. And I've got a job. A big job. Right here in the city. And the best part is the way I got it. I just reached right in there and took it out of that son of a bitch's hands."

"What son of a bitch?"

"It's a done deal. I know it."

"You sign the papers?"

Joe's eyes gleamed and he waved his arms as if to embrace the world, but there was a darkness beneath his exuberance. They knew my brother up here in the park. Sometimes he would buy a joint or two and sit on one of the benches, sharing the dope with whoever walked by, old hippies or gangbangers or ex-cons tattooed with the image of the Holy Virgin, the air around them thick with the smell of that sweet blue smoke. Though some people might think such low-lifing would get him in trouble, I didn't have much objection. Because it was not too long ago when Joe frequented the other end of the park, under the pepper trees, where the coke dealers liked to hang out, and he'd about ruined himself there. He'd been running his own crew then too, highballing it on luxury homes out in Woodside; then the money got out of control, and it all came crashing down. He'd even gone to Micaeli Romano for help but the old judge had been unable, or unwilling.

Joe handed me the joint and I took another hit and the sky seemed suffused with both beauty and danger. Dolores Park is in the shadow of the city's biggest hill so the fog rolls to either side and overhead there is that clear and startling blue. The sky today was calm in an ancient, dreamy way but I could feel too the violence in that dreaminess.

"I'll show you the property," my brother said.

We drove into the flatlands of the barrio, where the Indians used to hide from the Franciscans, and now the cranksters and the young gangbangers postured up and down Mission Street. Meanwhile, the sisters and mothers of these boys wandered through the zapaterías and grocerías, the streets boomed with the staccato rapping of the lowrider's radios, the sidewalks blossomed with color, the stench of overripe fruit, perfume, urine and feces, cinnamon rolls in outdoor booths where a little boy held a toy gun in one hand and with the other clutched at his mama's skirts, hiding himself in her giant haunches.

"We stopping by your place?"

"No. Do you want to stop by my place?"

"It doesn't matter."

"Then why do you ask?"

"We seem to be going that direction."

"Do you want to see Luisa, the kids?"

"No. It's okay."

"I want to show you this property. It will get dark if we don't go now."

"That's what want I to do. Let's see the property."

"You don't like my house? You don't like Luisa, the kids?"

"Stop it."

We made a joke out of it but the truth was I was glad not to go by his house. Luisa had been good to my brother but she gave me the cold shoulder anytime I walked through the door. I did not know why, but this was the way she'd always been to me—and Joe seemed to take pleasure in her rudeness. So we drove toward the bay into an industrial dis-

24

trict that had been built upon sludge and landfill and through which the Southern Pacific had run line after line of railroad tracks, a switching yard wider across than the Bayshore Freeway. The tracks were still there, though rusted orange with disuse. The place was called China Basin because of the coolies who had laid those tracks and lived in shanties nearby.

"This is it."

"There's nothing here."

"You have no vision, Nick. Can't you see? They're gonna build condos here, up and down. Office space, housing projects, playgrounds, all up and down. I've got a bid on the framing contract, for the residential end. And I'm going to get it. I know."

"How do you know?"

"Micaeli Romano's behind this deal. His law firm, the holding company, they're arranging the financing."

"I didn't know you two were friendly."

"We're not. But I've got some leverage."

"What kind of leverage?"

"The old man's done something he's not proud of. He doesn't want people to know."

"What are you trying to say?"

"Just what I said. Three-story condos, little boxes one on top the other. Redwood deck on the back. Garage underneath. It's as easy as they get. I can make myself some real money, then I can get out of here. Get myself something in Los Gatos, Monte Sereno. Nothing fancy. Just a place."

"You taking Luisa with you?"

"Sure," he said, but I did not think this had anything to do with Luisa. I could see the dreamy glint in my brother's eye, the kind of look men get when they think about what their life might have been. For my brother, Joseph Abruzzi Jones, it was those dry hills south of here where you could sit on your porch and all but imagine the ocean and the palms somewhere behind you and an orchard that rolled down the peninsula all the way to the bay. Of course there weren't any orchards anymore, and even the little stucco bungalows were being torn down for bigger homes, on land that sold for a million bucks an acre. My brother knew all this but it didn't matter. He still had that look in his eye.

"Eldorado Condominiums," he laughed. "That's the ticket. And I got the goods."

I laughed too but I felt a chill in my heart. Though I hadn't admitted it to myself, I'd seen a little door open in my life the day before at Jimmy Wong's. Standing on the other side of the door had been Micaeli Romano and the job Jimmy talked about. And maybe there had been other things behind that door too. Maybe in that land behind the door it was no longer true that what was good for me was bad for my brother. Maybe Micaeli Romano was the man everybody thought he was, and a sweet life awaited me. But none of that mattered either. Because to open that door and walk through and stand on the other side with Micaeli Romano, that was the stuff of betrayal.

"He's quite the stud, that Micaeli," said Joe.

"You mean his son?"

"I mean Micaeli."

"In his day, maybe. He's an old man now."

"A rich son of a bitch like him, it's always his day. But not anymore."

I turned my back on Joe and walked down the old railway track. The twilight was coming on, the skyline darkening, and I could see fog rolling in over North Beach.

"You're going to blackmail Micaeli Romano?" I laughed and filled my mouth with scorn. "That's a good one." Then I spit in the dirt and walked back to the car.

Joe stood outside a long time with his back to me, staring out at China Basin. Then he came back and slid behind the wheel. I pretended to be looking at the city, but of course I could feel his big, thick-shouldered presence in the car beside me, and the air was stuffy with the smell of us. It was the Abruzzi smell, or Jones, whoever the fuck we were, and it was the smell of my mother's food and my father stewing in his failure. I met my brother's eyes but just as quickly I looked away.

"You slept with her, didn't you, Nick?" he asked. "Right before the divorce?"

I cracked the window to let in a little bit of air. The

glass had misted with our breathing. I thought of the fogged windows of my mother's kitchen, and I thought about the times Joe and Marie and Anne and I had sat at that table, and how later, after he'd broken with Marie, I'd watched him smash the glass out of those kitchen windows with his fist.

"You slept with Marie, didn't you?" Joe asked again. I did not know why this was coming up now. I let the pause lengthen, too long maybe, then I looked him in the eye.

"No," I said.

He turned his head, thinking. "I am going to get that son of a bitch," he said at last.

"You do that," I said.

Then I went home and got drunk. I wandered the late-night streets with the Chinks and the hobos and the too-drunk tourists, all the nobodies of Columbus Avenue. Hunching under the neon light, they had learned the true secret of life, it seemed to me, and I wanted to be like them, wise as hell, immune from all desire.

FIVE
LINDA STREET

I got a call in the morning. I let it ring five times, six, then figured they wouldn't let it stop. The call woke me from my dreams, or that's the way I remember things now. There had not been any people in those dreams, it had just been shades of blue, large shapes that slid past one another in a larger and vaster darkness of blue, gun metal blue, midnight blue, blue fading into black, like the color of this prison cell late at night when my eyes are open and remembering the past is like a plunge into the life of another man.

"Mr. Jones?" The woman had a sad, official voice. She was with the San Francisco Police.

"Yes."

"Mr. Niccolò Jones?"

"Yes," I said again. Then she gave me the news. My brother was dead.

There had been a shooting, she told me, and the victim's driver's license carried the name of Joseph Jones. The incident occurred on the corner of Linda and Nineteenth, a few blocks from his residence. (A drug-dealing corner, I knew, a balmy little alley littered with scraps of plastic wrap. I listened for the innuendo in the woman's voice. Cocaine. Speed. It was a highballer's corner.) The department had spoken to a woman named Luisa Jones, but she had become hysterical when it came to identifying the victim. Before homicide released the body from forensics to the mortuary, the department needed definitive identification.

The lady cop told me this in a sweet, blue-eyed way, like a nurse repeating a cancer diagnosis. I imagined her sitting behind a desk, and I could hear the starched white blouse in her voice and see the forms stacked neatly to the side.

"I'll be down in a little while," I said.

My voice sounded like somebody else's, a nice guy's maybe, somebody's husband with an errand to do after work. But I was thinking of my brother and those pictures you see of corpses being wheeled into metal drawers at the city morgue.

28

I know when someone dies all of a sudden you are supposed to be struck with disbelief. Maybe this is how it struck me. I know I fell back on my bed and clutched at my head and moaned like a gangster in a bad movie, an actor making a ploy for the audience's sympathy. At the same time though I felt a surge of joy at my core and this same joy caused a misery in my heart, an awfulness. I wretched and I sobbed. I know my pain was not like you are supposed to feel. Rather it was something else, some kind of gangster pain. There was a harsh light coming through the window and I could see the motes of dust floating in its slanted rays. The traffic made an ugly noise outside.

I had slept in my shirt, in the stink and grime of the day before, and I could still smell all that on my body, and I could taste too the smoke and booze in my throat. I went into the shower to wash it off. I spent a long time under the hot, steaming water, lathering myself, washing away the soap then starting again from the top. I washed myself clean maybe a dozen times, even after the water had turned cold and I had begun to shiver under the spray.

There was a mirror on the bathroom door, and when I got out of the shower I looked my dripping body up and down. My brother and I have always looked pretty much alike, head to toe, including the extra weight about the gut. I studied the face up close. It was the same face, more or less, that I would see again just a few hours later, when the cops pulled back the white cloth and gave me a peek at my brother's corpse.

That afternoon I went to the downtown station and met with homicide detective Leanora Chinn. I told her I was a lawyer so she gave me the autopsy report and the pictures and all the details that the voice this morning had been too discreet to mention over the phone.

My brother had been shot at close range, close enough for powder burns on the chest, and he had been hurled backwards by the bullet, straight back, so he fell onto the pavement with both arms outstretched. It was a small-caliber gun, so he had taken a few minutes to die there on the street, clasping and unclasping his hand while blood gushed up his throat. Technically the medics were unable to determine whether death was due to loss of blood or asphyxiation due to blood in the mouth, but the officer's handwriting summed it up on the form in the appropriate box. Gunshot Wound to the Heart. There were no suspects in the case, Chinn told me, but police had gone door-to-door and had reason, because of the location, to suspect it was a drug deal gone bad. There were crack vials nearby and the victim's wallet, riffled and empty of money, lay in the street.

"At least that's the way the case stands now," Chinn said. The formality in her voice, mixed with the sadness, made me realize what had escaped me till that moment. She was the same woman who had called me earlier this morning on the phone.

"My brother wasn't buying drugs. Not on Linda Street, anyway," I told Chinn.

She did not look like the woman I had imagined. Her shirt was neither starched nor white, but blue—and she wore a badge over the pocket. Her hair was black and she wore it cut blunt.

"He had problems with coke once, but that was over. I don't think this had anything to do with drugs."

Chinn nodded and jotted the words *prior user* at the bottom of the form. Then she turned me over to the man in the white coat, the coroner, who took me through several doorways down corridors that smelled increasingly of formaldehyde and at last to a gurney wheeled into a corner against the wall. I didn't need to look, I knew it was Joe by the shape of his big toe protruding out from under the sheet. I went through the motions anyway and stood there at attention while the man peeled back the cloth.

The features were slack, lips pale, face drained of color, a short stubble on the cheeks. The man lying there didn't look any way Joe had ever looked when he was alive, but it was still him, his bones and his face.

"Yeah," I said. "That's my brother."

I nodded my head and tried to blink the image away, but I saw my dead brother's face again, or something close, in the window glass as I walked down the hall—and I saw it again when I glanced into the rearview mirror in the station parking lot. I started the car but I didn't put it in gear. Instead I thought of Joe standing out on the corner of Linda Street and how he'd probably gotten a glimpse of the gun before the killer pushed it against his chest and left him staring at the black sky. I dwelled the moment over, imagining the violent whooze in his head, the plummeting of the stars, the blood rising in his throat. I lit a cigarette, inhaling deep, too deep, feeling first the rise of nausea, then a needling sensation on my skin. I wanted to get back to North Beach and have a drink. As I pulled out of the lot I caught sight of Leanora Chinn sitting on the station steps. Something in the way she sat there made me guess she had been watching me for some time. Watching in the way that cops watch, pretending she didn't see you at all, with something else on her mind.

That night I went to visit Luisa. No one was answering the phone at her place, and I knew her opinion of me was not a high one, but there are times when people are bound together, like it or not, and I felt the need to walk into my brother's house and get a look at the things of his everyday life.

Luisa was born in a village outside Mazatlán and had two children before she was twenty, then managed to drag both herself and her children north. Who had fathered her children, if it had been one man or two, or whether she had married either of them, these were questions to which I did not know the answer and never asked. I used to think Luisa did not love my brother but had married him when he was at rock bottom, vulnerable, because she was an illegal and wanted permanent residence. Maybe that had been true at first. She'd been only twenty-two then, and my brother had seemed the fool walking about with this young Mexican woman under his arm, especially if you knew about Marie and how Joe had torn up the dirt when she left him. But

Luisa had stayed with my brother. She had not run off when her status came through.

When I knocked on the door now, I saw in the window that she was on her knees before the Santeria shrine in her living room.

My brother and Luisa's place was one of those damp little Victorians in the Mission, painted a bright yellow on the outside, but inside it smelled of dry rot. Like houses up and down the street, it had been built on backfilled marsh, so the land was inherently wet and nothing could be done. The rooms inside the house were lined up shotgun style, one behind another, a long hall to the side. Light did not penetrate to the end of that hall. There was a little concrete yard in the rear where some bougainvillea grew, and beyond this was a cyclone fence strung with concertina wire to keep out the crackheads who lived in the house behind. A radio blasted a Mexican polka two doors down, some kids wailed, and the evening carried with it the smell of night jasmine and cooking grease.

I knocked on the door. When no one answered, I pushed the door open and peered in. Luisa still knelt in front of her shrine. She had covered its altar with candles, placing among them a picture of my brother and a doll fashioned into his likeness. At the feet of this doll were bits of sawdust, glue, old nails, the tools of Joe's profession, a candle melted into the shape of a devil—its purpose being to scare away the devil, I guess—and feathers and trinkets and a statue of Jesus with His arms spread like Joe's arms had been spread when the cops snapped his photo on the pavement. Luisa rocked and moaned, oblivious to me, carrying on in the fashion of old Italian women I had seen in my childhood. Though whatever superstition those old women may have practiced, they did so alone and out of sight because this was America and that was 1956 and they'd been ashamed of their ignorance even if they could not help themselves and had no desire to change.

I went quietly past Luisa, upstairs to my brother's room. Though everything in the police report pointed otherwise, I did not want to believe he had been down on Linda Street chasing that cheap rock. He was an impulsive son of a bitch, Joe was, but he was no crackhead. Or at least that's what I wanted to think right then. The evidence of his good intentions seemed all around me. In the shape of his clothes hanging in his bedroom closet. In the angle of his shoes there at the foot of the bed. In the papers and paraphernalia scattered over the top of his dresser.

I shuffled through my brother's papers, thinking I might find something to tell me what he'd been doing on Linda Street. All I found were some old pictures, and also some newspaper clippings from the real estate section. They were the type of things he was always clipping, advertisements for developments in progress, sketches of custom homes, the kind of jobs he'd run in the old days. On the back of one of those ads—over the local obituaries—he had scrawled some figures. They made no sense to me, and I pushed the papers away.

I was more interested in one of the photos, a picture taken twelve, maybe fifteen years back. Joe and Marie and myself down at Ocean Beach, before Playland was torn down, so you could see the amusement center in the background and the Ferris wheel spinning around. Marie was in the center. She held each of us by the hand and we all leaned back together against Joe's convertible. Joe and I looked awkward as hell but Marie looked triumphant. It must have been Anne who took the picture, I guessed. There was no evidence of her anywhere but that's the way it would be.

In the picture Joe wore a jacket of mine, a blue corduroy thing that he had worn a lot then because Marie liked the looks of it on him. I had seen it on him lately, when he was in a reminiscent kind of mood. I put the picture in my pocket and went back to his closet, hunting for the jacket. It had been mine before it had been his, after all, but more than that I liked being in his closet, heavy with the smell of him. It was the same reason maybe that Luisa had gathered bits and pieces of him to put downstairs on her altar. I found the jacket in his closet and put it on. It was a little heavier than it should have been, with a lilt to one side, but I did not take much notice of this at first. I looked in the mirror and decided, yes, I would take the jacket. It was a bit worn and it fit badly but I would take it. Then I put my hand in the pocket and came out with a gun.

It was a small revolver, its barrel rubbed with blueing so it was the color I have told you about in my dreams. I did not know much about guns, but I spun the barrel and could see it was loaded. I knew Joe kept a gun for self-protection but at that moment I thought other things too. Maybe someone had been after Joe. He had been in trouble, and the police were wrong about everything. My ideas were half-formed and contradictory and so were my emotions. I shoved the gun back in the jacket pocket and started downstairs.

As I left the room, though, I noticed Joe's papers. I'd left them scattered over the top of his dresser. I started to put the newspaper clippings back where I'd found them; but—at the last moment—I grabbed and took them too.

Downstairs, Luisa still knelt at the altar. She was disheveled and the strap that held her dress had started to fall off the shoulder. She lifted her head, hearing me and turning as if in a trance, rising from her knees and smiling, moist-eyed, momentarily overwhelmed with some miraculous joy. Then I realized what had happened and in that same instant, she realized it too.

She had mistaken me for my brother. But no, her prayers had not been answered. Joe Abruzzi had not returned from the dead.

"What are you doing? That's not your jacket."

"I let Joe borrow it. A long time ago."

"Why do you come in my house and sneak up behind me?" she asked. "I know all about you, what kind of man."

"Was Joe doing coke?"

"If you were a true brother, you wouldn't ask such a thing."

"Then what was he doing on Linda Street?"

She had no answer for this and it could be that no one had any answer, that he'd just been out for a walk, shot dead by coincidence, an addicted fuck, a teenage wannabe, a mugger who thought a gun was a prick and jerked off by watching it flash in his hand. Luisa knew all this too, though she knew it in Spanish, in the language of the shrine.

She gave me a look like when Joe was still alive and she wanted me gone from her house.

"I know about you."

"What do you know?"

She cocked her hips a little, I cocked mine, and the air was charged with a lurid expectancy. It showed in my eyes, maybe, and in hers, and in the very slope of our bodies. I turned my face away, ashamed at what was in my head, but I could not help but glance back at her, checking her up, and when I did she glared at me in disgust.

"How are you and the kids set?" I asked. "Maybe I could help out."

It was a lie of course. I didn't have any money in the world and she knew this. Besides, she had her friends and the community around her, and after the funeral she and her two kids named Julia and Juarez Jones would disappear into that great other population of California the newspapers and television always mentioned but seemed to know nothing about. Out into the valleys of walnuts and cottonwoods and dried grass where the immigrants speak in a thousand tongues, building cities out of materials too vile and wonderful to imagine. I wished I could disappear into that other world too, but the magic hour for people like me had long passed.

"I talked to the Green Street Mortuary," I said, one hand on the door handle. "And everything's cleared with the police. The funeral's in three days."

I walked over to Linda Street, to the corner where my brother had been shot. There is a small playground there, a mural on the cement wall, blood-red colors, hanging fruit, a pregnant woman, a field laborer, her womb blousy and gauzelike, and through that gauze you could see the growing child. The dealers were trading beneath the mural. There was some of that yellow police ribbon lying about on the ground, and a chalk outline of my brother's corpse on the white pavement where he had fallen, and that chalk had already begun to smear and fade. I sat down on one of the curbs and a dealer approached me. His eyes widened as he came near, he faltered a step, and it occurred to me that my brother's picture had been in the afternoon paper and maybe the young dealer saw the resemblance, as Luisa had seen it, and thought I was my own brother come back from the grave. Then he came forward anyway. He was a business man first and foremost, and any sale was a good sale, even to a ghost.

"Smack?" he asked. "Bag cocaine?"

"No, thank you."

My voice was polite as hell. I buried my head in my hands and looked for the grief deep in there, buried under all those layers of dark. It took a while but then I found it and sobbed into my hands with all those dealers watching, juggling their rocks in their big-ass pockets, whistling at the moon.

SIX
THE TRIGGER

Not long after I arrived here in Coldwater, I stopped paying attention to my surroundings. I learned how to ignore everything and to be watchful at the same time. There is farmland beyond the walls of the prison, I know this, and beyond the walls too are neat little stucco houses and palm trees and roads that lead to those houses, and it's true that sometimes I imagine myself walking down one of those roads. Perhaps someone whispers my name, and I hear the voice of Homicide Detective Leanora Chinn, and I walk beside her straight and true.

I don't mean to suggest I have lost touch with reality. Partly it is a way of acting. The other prisoners leave me alone. Not out of fear or respect or some notion of human dignity, but because I have managed to adopt the manner of a fixture, a person who blends into the ordinariness of a place and its routine. Everything they say about prisons is true, just as it is true that men here, as in other occupations of life, survive by holding themselves aloof. At night I hear the other prisoners roll about in their cots. I hear them moan and know they are masturbating and know too that their cell mates go on reading, or picking their toes, or whatever it is they do to get by. Because we have seen what happens when that aloofness is dropped. Maybe two cell mates touch one another and begin to kiss. I see the small red flare of a cigarette, forbidden after lights out, and smell the sweetsick smell of the tobacco, and am overwhelmed maybe with my own hunger and a sense of fear, because that small grunt might not be pleasure at all but the sound a man makes when he is muffled about the throat, then stabbed with a kitchen spoon that has been filed into another shape altogether. When two men want the same thing, when desire seeks physical expression, these are our problems. So I act as if I do not hear. I close my eyes and drift to the edge of sleep, past the infinite shades of blue, dreaming of my other life until I am on the streets of North Beach again, and this prison cell is a shadow world.

*   *   *

When I got home I took my brother's gun and stashed it way back in my bottom drawer, underneath clothes which I never wore. I looked at the newspaper clippings, and still could make nothing of them, and after a while I figured there was nothing to be made. It was just Joe, looking for work, and the clippings revealed about as much of importance as the obituaries of the old Italians over which he'd scribbled his notes. I told myself, though, that there would be other leads to follow. I held in my head the vague notion I would somehow solve the mystery of my brother's death.

The next morning an article appeared in *The Chronicle*, a short little item in the crime section, in which the reporter let himself wax eloquent. "For Joseph Abruzzi Jones the hard times came to an end two nights ago, when the 38-year-old North Beach native was shot dead in a drug deal in the Mission."

I did not particularly like this spin on events and was brooding over it when I got a call from Jimmy Wong, pissed off because I'd missed filing a deadline on some Russian refugees he wanted me to evict. I didn't feel much like talking to Wong. I gave him the silent treatment and let him hang there on the phone.

"What's the matter with you, Abruzzi?"

"I'm busy."

"What do you mean, busy?"

"I've got appointments, Jimmy. I got some dagos to evict. One o'clock sharp. Chinks at two. Jiggaboos at three. A man has to keep busy."

Then I hung it up.

I paced back and forth, grubbing around in my emotions, in the guilt over things I had done, or imagined I'd done, or maybe not done at all when I should've, but didn't have the nerve. Instead I'd lingered in the old neighborhood, not getting out but not staying either, not really, always lingering on the edge.

I wasn't going to do that anymore, I told myself. Though what I was going to do instead I had no idea.

38

I studied my brother's picture in the newspaper, figuring the case was all but closed now, the police were satisfied. I wanted to blame someone for what had happened but there was no one to blame except Joe himself or circumstance or maybe myself for being who I am. I took a drink, then I cursed all that crap and threw my glass against the wall.

SEVEN
OCEAN BEACH

We held the funeral out in South City, in the Italian Cemetery, where I'd gone often enough as a kid, when I was still in school and the old Italians of the neighborhood were dying off one by one. There had been green space between the graves then, an open meadow between the Italians and nearby Colma Cemetery. In the years since that time, the meadow had filled with graves, and the boundaries between the Italians and everyone else had disappeared.

My mother was buried up with the old Italians, because that's the way she wanted it, but my father was in a VA plot the other side of the hill. We were laying Joe somewhere in-between, alongside a family whose name was Panarelli on one side and Merriwether on the other.

Only a handful came to the burial. Luisa's kids laid some red Mexican roses, the color of lips, over my brother's casket, and Father Campanelli read the passage from the book about the dust to the dust and the ash to the ash. Meanwhile, I looked over the meadow at the gray stones rising from the grass and the road rolling through the cemetery. A yellow taxi moved down that road, coming toward us. Luisa let out a little wail and the kids tilted against one another, lugubrious as hell, all but identical in their dark suits and linen collars.

After the priest had done his bit, we lowered my brother down. I tossed in the first shovel. Campanelli and the funeral people tried to lead us away then, because this was the moment known as the twilight moment, when the grave was still open, the family vulnerable, and widows most likely to hurl themselves in. Luisa would not leave but she did not hurl herself either. She stood at the edge of things watching the grave diggers do their work. She held a spray of roses in her hands and she would wait, I guessed, until the grave was tamped and packed, then she would place the flowers on the dirt.

By this time the taxi had stopped and a woman had gotten out, standing way back among the willows. It was

Marie. She watched us from a distance. I waited a beat or two, then decided to head in her direction. Father Campanelli choose that moment to put his hand on my shoulder.

"How are things with you, Nick?" His voice was thick. We had known each other since I was a kid.

"I'm doing well. Things considered."

"If you need someone to talk to?"

The old priest's eyes were rheumy and tired. He still kept the old calm, though, and had about him the smell of black cloth and incense that reminded me of the altar and those days long ago when I confessed to him all my sins, leaving out only how I walked around with my dick so hard that it was all I could do not to fall down and screw the dirt. Rumor was the old priest had prostate cancer now.

"I dedicated this morning's mass to your brother."

"Thank you, Father."

"I'll say another tomorrow."

"I appreciate that."

I glanced up toward Marie, then he glanced too and saw what was drawing me away.

"You'll come see me?"

The way his voice quavered I could not be sure if he meant for religious purposes or because he was an old man and just wanted to talk. It didn't matter. He knew I was going to give him the brush. It was how you had to be with a priest.

"Sure," I said. "I'll come by the chapel."

I hurried through the cemetery, snaking through the stones, with Marie up ahead, and behind me the long sound of the dirt falling into my brother's grave. I could feel Campanelli watching me and didn't like the feeling. He knew why I was hurrying, I guessed. With all the confessions he'd heard over the years, there wasn't much he didn't know about what went on in North Beach. I reached Marie, but when I turned the old priest was gone. It was just Luisa watching the diggers now. Her two kids played tag among the graves.

"Is that Joe's wife?" asked Marie.

"Yeah. That's Luisa. She's not crazy about me."

41

"Why not?"

"Joe told her some things. About you and me, during your divorce. That's what I think."

"He didn't know about that."

"Joe had his suspicions," I said.

Marie was dressed in black. She wore a black kerchief too over her blonde hair and her lips were red like an apple. Her skin did not seem so olive as it had once been, but rather to have grown fair with the years, almost white. The sight of her up close startled my heart and the feelings were the same as they'd always been, only rawer and without much sense of innocence about them. I wanted to be with her, to drive her home, so I went over and paid the taxi driver his fare.

"Can you afford that?" she asked.

"No. But you always were extravagant."

"Is that what you think? That I live an extravagant life?"

"Compared to some. Anyway, we haven't seen each other much these last years, you and me."

"I didn't know if I should come to the funeral."

"There weren't many people to object, were there?"

"His wife."

"She didn't see you."

We climbed in my car and drove up Cemetery Avenue to the freeway, where above you the row houses of Daly City sweep over the hills, one line after the other, while below the gravestones tumble like dominoes toward the bay.

"When you get down to it," I said, "Joe was happy with simple things. He didn't want much."

"That's not true. Your brother wanted plenty."

"He wanted you."

"Well, he got me, didn't he?"

"When was the last time you saw him?"

"A couple weeks back. He stopped by to talk."

"You two never let off, did you?"

She didn't answer and I felt all the old tension between us, the ugly stuff. It wasn't the way I wanted things to be. When the road crowned I took the next exit, onto the Sunset

Highway. The wind was blowing hard and up above you could see the place where the weather changed and the fog billowed up under the blue edge of the sky. From here the clouds were a dark, blustering gray all the way to ocean.

"Where are we going?" she asked.

"Ocean Beach."

We looked at each other a long moment, and I found myself taking in the full angle of her face, and I saw the age that was starting to appear, and I realized she wasn't going to say yes or no, and that everything was up to me. I felt our car vanishing into a stream of cars, all of us rolling along on the road between the houses and the graves.

The breeze was harder down by the ocean and harder yet when we got to the other side of the sea wall. Though it was late July, summer on this side of the city is as bad as winter and the ocean had that bitter look. Behind us the abandoned windmills at the edge of the park cut a shadow against the sky, and in front of us the sand was filigreed with a yellow foam. Clumps of wood and refuse had washed onto the beach; down current there was heavy equipment, tractors and cranes digging a trench for new sewage pipes that would take all the junk and refuse and crap of San Francisco and deposit it a dozen miles further out. The pipes they used now were not long enough—and when the current was wrong, everything came washing back to shore.

Marie tightened her coat around her.

"The police think it was a street thing," I said. "Some kind of drug deal gone bad, but I don't believe that. Things were going well for Joe. He had some work lined up."

"Maybe," Marie said.

She looked out at the gray ocean, the gray sky, the gray rocks, and it was suddenly all too goddamned gray for me.

"There's things you never saw when you looked at your brother. You didn't know everything."

"What are you trying to tell me? The cops are right?"

The seagulls were cawing above us, the pelicans screeching, and the sound of a bull seal echoed out from the rocks.

"Son of a bitch," she said and began to sob, a little at

first, her arms hanging loose under her long coat, and I went up and put my arms around her, but carefully, so that we did not touch too close. She seemed far away, lost in her own swelling grief, and I was remote from her until at last she leaned into me, and I felt the relief, all her grief coming out, and noticed too the scent of her hair and the softness of her body, and she was crying harder now, and I felt looking out at the ocean the great waves building and building, so that the tears rolled a little down my face too, and the salt taste was in my mouth. I imagined my brother as a child and saw how he looked, smiling at me, and I clutched Marie more tightly, suddenly aware of her body in a way I had tried not to think of, at least not right now, but I could tell she was aware of my body too, and my lips touched the crook of her neck. She pulled away so that I was looking into her dark eyes and she was looking into mine. Then I kissed her, a wild kiss, and she kissed me back, a kiss sinful and innocent at the same time, with the taste of something unspeakable. Then we let each other go and stood staring down at our feet, where the water had rushed up, then receded, and the yellow scum was floating on the sand.

EIGHT
THE SEARCH BEGINS

The next day I put on my dirtiest clothes and fancied out into the Mission, looking for my brother's murderer. I am not sure what got into me; it wasn't the kind of thing I usually did. I told myself I didn't believe the police explanation. Maybe that was part of it. Maybe, though, it had something to do with the way Luisa had treated me before the funeral and the lousy way that made me feel. I wanted to prove to myself I was a good brother, and the way to prove that was to wander around the streets of the Mission, a picture of Joseph Abruzzi Jones in my pocket. I thought I might find somebody who'd seen him on the street the night he died, or at least find out if he'd been on the slide again, like the police seemed to think.

I went back to Dolores Park, down into the hollow under the pepper trees, and squatted on a bench there in front of an outdoor table. Some young men loitered under a statue nearby, kicking at the pigeons, and it didn't take long. One of them, a Mexican kid—his body thin like a rake, chest concave—sauntered over and sat down across from me.

"Cocaine?" I asked.

"I have weed, hash. Good herb. No coke."

"I want coke."

"Wait a minute. I get my friend. He meet you at that table over there. Forty bucks for a rock, but you don't smoke it here. Smoke it someplace else. Now give me the money."

That was the way the kids worked their business. One took your money, strolled away, then one of his buddies met you with the drugs. They kept the stuff stashed somewhere nearby, working it so nobody was holding it for very long and it was tough for the cops to make a sting.

I reached as if to pull money from my wallet but instead I took out a picture of my brother, then laid a couple bills out across it.

"I don't want the coke. I want the man who sells the

coke. I want to know if he knows my brother, in the picture."

The kid glanced down.

"Fuck you," he said.

Then he sauntered back to his friends. They talked me over in Spanish for a while, and laughed, kicking at the pigeons. A customer came up and I watched them go through the routine with a new guy, this time selling a couple of joints. After that they ignored me, or pretended to, and I began to feel as if I were fading into the invisible world. So I went down to Linda Street, to try the dealers there, and got the same treatment more or less, only now someone was following me. A white man, hair the color of oil, wearing a black blazer and long black tie. I saw him again outside Picaro's, a bohemian cafe where management didn't bother to chase off the junkies who wandered in every fifteen seconds begging for change. They were part of the local charm.

I gave the junkies nickels and quarters, showing them the picture of my brother, and at last some old junkie older than death itself told me he thought maybe he'd seen my brother in the El Corazón, a movie theater that had been converted to a hotel ten years back, and these days that hotel was a crack palace first class. The man who would know for sure, the old junkie said, was in room 21.

So I headed to Mission Street. The man in the blazer still followed me, eating a burrito as he walked, licking his fingers, not seeming to care if he was conspicuous or no. I ignored him and clumped up the rotting stairs of the El Corazón, then down a long hall to the back of the building. At the end was number 21 and inside I found a surly little man in a white t-shirt. The man's arms were tattooed and his hair stood up in a lick, wet and ugly, as if a cow had dragged its tongue over his head.

"You looking for some jewel?"

I went through the same routine again, taking out my wallet and the picture.

"This is my brother."

"I got one of my baby sister. You wanna trade?"

"I want to know if you ever seen him."

"The cops already been round here with this. And I told them the same thing I'll tell you; I ain't never seen this brother of yours."

"An old junkie, he told me he'd seen him here."

"I know that junkie. He's full of shit. Now you want some jewel? If no, then I don't have dick for you. *Capisch?*"

"I understand."

"I got me a business here. Free enterprise. Lai-zay faire. I don't want any trouble."

The little man sat behind a desk, his hand inside one of the drawers. If I gave him any trouble I guessed he would shoot me, then take his drugs and his money and disappear down the fire escape. Or maybe he would just flush the drugs and tell the cops I was some kind of burglar broke into his room in broad daylight, come to steal his cowlick.

I turned to the door.

"Hey?"

"Yeah?"

"Your picture."

I went back to the desk to pick it up but the man stopped my hand, gandering all over the photograph. His eyes went sentimental all of a sudden, his face slack, soft as a peach. Then he let it go.

"No, your brother ain't never came around this place. But I tell you, I know how it feels. You want some jewel, I give you a break. One time."

"Thanks a ton."

I walked down the hall, thinking what a swell guy he was, and as I walked past those hall doors, one after another, I noticed all of them were shut. I could hear some godawful moaning behind them, and laughing. I was glad not to know what was going on inside.

Outside, the man in the blazer was gone. I looked around for a place to have a beer, or something to eat, but then I looked around again, up and down those streets, and felt a dirty wave of anguish wash up into my gut. My brother was dead and I would never find anything I needed in the Mission. These people would never help me. I walked down to Capp Street, past the little immigrant boys who sold their bodies for ice cream and candy, and I kept walking, all the way down Market, through the thickening crowd, until I was back home in North Beach. I walked past the familiar bars along Broadway, where everything seemed to me somehow simpler and more wholesome: just girls in G-strings and giggling tourists and old men beating off into the Naugehyde.

I bought myself a can of beer from the corner store and sat on a stoop outside the Dante Hotel, looking across at the naked lights of the strip joints and at the hawkers out front, those fat little men in ribbed shirts and black slacks, bouncing up and down, trying to steer the passersby inside. In the middle of the block was a place called J. Ferrari's, which was nothing from the outside but a blank door and a window whose glass had been spray-painted black.

It was an easy place to miss, and the only reason I noticed it now was because a small, monkey-faced man emerged from inside. People in the neighborhood called him J. Ferrari because that was the name stenciled on the window, but the truth was that that lettering was very old and the ugly little man was only in his thirties. I did not know his real name, but I knew Ferrari's had been a bookie joint when I was a kid, and that even now the sleaze joints and restaurants up and down the block paid rent to the little man. Though the *prominenti* denied it, people around the neighborhood said part of that money went back to some old mobster in Chicago, and they told you too that Ferrari's was the place to go if you ever wanted to have someone's fingers cut off, or if you wanted your wife to disappear into the bay, and that had always been so and always would be, so long as there was an Italian in North Beach. I'd got a look inside J. Ferrari's once, and it was nothing at all, just a small room with a desk, though I'd heard rumors there was a hidden door in the wall, leading into the bowels of the building, and from there you could follow the old tunnels into Chinatown. I did not know if any of that was true, but I did know I'd seen Chinese stopping by his office, same as Italians.

None of that mattered to me though, because the monkey man was not my problem, and I wanted to get myself a drink.

I crossed the street and was starting in serious at the bar. After a while a little girl named Suzie came and sat beside me. She was half-Filipino, half-black, and half-Italian, she told me, the daughter of an American soldier, born in captivity, and she wanted to give me a blow job. I put my arm around her and stumbled out into the street; then I gave her a few bucks and a little kiss on the cheek and told her to go away.

"Not tonight, Suzie."

"Too late. You already pay."

"What you mean?"

"You got time coming. You deal with me, you get what you deserve."

I was sky drunk and didn't understand. Two men rushed at me from the mouth of the alley, big men, and though neither of them was the man in the blazer, I thought of him anyway and believed he had somehow tracked me down. I had done myself stupid, I thought, going down to the Mission, fucking around where I shouldn't fuck. I tried to run but I was too drunk and big tears were rolling out of my eyes. They caught me and threw me against the wall. One of them held my arms behind my back, the other one snapped on cuffs, the little girl stood nearby watching, hands on her hips—and suddenly it came clear to me. I had been wrong. These weren't thugs, these were vice, all three of them. The girl was no little girl at all but a cop, and now they were going to take me down for solicitation. They pulled out my wallet, looking for identification, and one of the cops recognized the name.

"Abruzzi Jones," he said. "This guy's brother was just shot down in the Mission."

"Look at those tears."

"Poor son-of-a-bitch."

"It's a rotten place, this world."

"Hey," protested Suzie. "It's not that rotten. He broke the law."

"It'll never stick. The judges in this city, they're all soft hearts."

"Or perverts."

"Oh, fuck you guys!" said Suzie. "You go in there. See if you like their fat hands on your thighs."

The men ignored Suzie. Out of the milk of human kindness, or because they were a little drunk themselves, they let me go. They pushed me out of the alley and told Suzie to go back inside, this one was no good, a weeper and a wailer, and please go back and find someone whose brother hadn't just been shot through the heart.

NINE
LEANORA CHINN

The next day I got a call from Lieutenant Chinn. The investigation was ongoing and she needed a few minutes of my time.

"Odds and ends," she explained.

"Should I come down?"

"No. I'll be out in the neighborhood today. Your place, I'll stop by."

I thought Leanora Chinn arranged it that way to be polite, to spare me a trip to the station. After she knocked on my door, though, I realized the other reason; she wanted to get a peek at me in my native habitat, to see what she could see. I sensed she was disappointed. The place was clean, or at least clean enough, and there wasn't any blood smeared on the walls.

She looked over some old photographs hanging by my desk. Relatives from Italy. The neighborhood in the old days. Marie and Joe and I, leaning against that car down at Ocean Beach, in that photo I'd swiped from my brother's place the day after he died.

"Family?"

"Yeah. My wall of ancestors."

Chinn peered into a shot of my mom and dad out on a Sunday stroll, striking a pose in front of Stephano's Garment Shop.

"That building's been torn down."

"Yeah, but Stephano's still going strong. Down on Union Square."

"I remember him. Needle and thread, cuffing everyone's pants."

"You from the neighborhood?"

"Yes," she said. "I live in the same house I grew up in."

I gave Lieutenant Chinn a second look. She had hard eyes, it was true, but she had small delicate lips, with a faint gloss on them, and she wore a straight skirt and a simple blouse, each one a different shade of blue. If you saw her on the street you might just think she was a Chinatown working girl, with her wholesome face and her quick walk, but the truth was, her clothes were police colors, even if they were not police uniform, and her eyes were black as her hair and unforgiving.

"This woman, Marie Donnatelli?" Lieutenant Chinn pointed to Marie in the picture.

"You know Marie?"

"I stopped by her apartment day before yesterday. Day of the funeral. I was parked in my car, across the street, when you dropped her off."

"Oh."

Chinn looked at me with those eyes of hers and I felt my chest tighten. Because before Marie climbed out of the car, she'd given me a quick sisterly kiss—as if to change the meaning of everything that had gone before—but I'd reached out and put my hand under her coat, fumbling, and Marie had let out a sweet little moan and buried her head in my shoulder.

"What was your relationship with Marie?"

"She was my brother's first wife."

"That part, I know."

"To be honest I haven't talked to her, nothing but a hello on the street, not for years. Then after the funeral, we took a drive around. We talked a little bit."

"You used to be lovers, didn't you?"

"Marie tell you that? Or Luisa?"

"Does it make any difference?"

"Probably not. Anyway, it was a long time ago. We were kids. It was before she married my brother."

"Before she married your brother?"

"Yes. Before."

"What kind of relationship did they have?"

"What do you mean?"

"Was it violent?"

"They had Latin tempers, if that's what you're asking. But it was only shouting and fuss. Nothing serious. Anyway, it was over between those two. There wasn't any reason for them to be fighting now."

"Are you sure?"

"Yeah."

"A neighbor in the complex told us there was an argument at Marie's apartment. Between a man and a woman, a couple of days before the murder."

"I wouldn't know anything about that."

"It got loud and ugly."

"Maybe it came from a different apartment."

I walked to the window and glanced down into the street, past the Naked Moon to Zirpoli's Books, where in the days before my time the neighborhood men would gather, smoking their cigars, and listen to Mussolini on the radio. Some hipsters hung out front now, posturing in their black sweatshirts and black jeans, tossing jibes at the tourists, mocking their polo shirts, their Midwestern pastels. Beyond them the gaudy lanterns of Chinatown receded up the hill.

Leonora Chinn stood behind me. She put something soft into her voice. "I grew up on this side of Grant, just a few blocks up."

"What school?"

"Galileo."

It was the same school as mine, only Leonora was a few years younger, one of those Chinese girls who clustered at the edge of the asphalt, back when the streets were Italian and the playgrounds too and God stuffed every piece of ravioli with a dollar bill. Two separate worlds, the Chinese and the Italians. Though we lived side by side, we kept our distance. The Chinese spoke their own language, or at least the old ones did, but they fell silent at your approach. I remember swaggering into that silence, but the longer I swaggered, the deeper that silence and the more I feared it would overwhelm me.

"We lived in Winter Alley," she said at last. "My family was one of the first to move across Broadway. 1965. The street was full of bougainvillea then."

"It was also full of Italians."

"Yes."

"They didn't like seeing you then, moving onto their street."

"They don't like seeing me now. A Chinese cop."

"Well, they've been here a long time. My parents came in the '30s. The old ones, before that."

"Mine came during the Gold Rush."

I did not want to get into this because I knew there was no way of getting out. Nobody forgets anything in this world. Because even if the mind forgets, the blood remembers. Just as the children of the long-dead Genovesi do not forget how the Sicilians drove their grandparents from Fisherman's Wharf, the Chinese do not forget how Sbarboro's Italian dragoons torched Chinatown, nor do the granddaughters of pigtailed fishmongers forget the faces of Italian kids who threw rocks through their windows late at night. I was one of those kids, I guess, just as I was a kid who stood on the corner and watched the Chinese girls, all dressed up, plaid skirts and skinny legs, disappear down alleys I'd been warned never to go.

"A plainclothes saw you down in the Mission at the El Corazón," said Leanora Chinn. "I don't think that's a great idea."

"The man in the blazer?"

"He said you were putting yourself at risk."

"Someone has to find my brother's murderer."

"Not you. Not in the Mission."

"I showed his picture around. No one recognized it."

"They're not going to tell you that. Besides, that picture looks as much like you."

"They'll think I'm his ghost," I said.

"They'll think you're a cop. You keep wandering around, you'll stumble into something, nothing to do with your brother, and someone will think you're after something that you're not, and you'll get hurt for no reason you care about, and it won't do anybody any good."

"It wasn't a drug deal. That wasn't why Joe was killed."

"Then why?"

"I don't know."

"Let me ask me you some other questions."

Then Lieutenant Chinn went down her list, reading off a little pad, all the while sitting with her knees close together, her feet crossed at the ankles. Who were my brother's enemies? Was he sleeping with anyone besides

Luisa? What were his business contacts? She went on like this more or less and I answered her questions. I don't think I helped her much. Then finally she stood up to go and told me I should leave the investigation to the police. I took that to mean they were writing it off as a street homicide, drug-related, or a robbery. I was almost relieved. I didn't want to think about it anymore.

Before she left, just before I took her hand to say good-bye, Leanora Chinn asked me another question.

"Where were you the night your brother was murdered?"

I should have known it was coming but I didn't, and now I felt a hard little noise in my chest, thumping out of tune.

"I was with him earlier that day. We had some drinks, drove around. I left him about seven."

"Where did you go after?"

"Here, to North Beach."

"Where were you between 10:00 and 10:30?"

"That the time of death?"

"Pretty close."

"I was here."

"Did anybody in the neighborhood see you?"

"The clerk down at the Corner Smoke. I went in for cigarettes. Before that I had dinner down at Jojo's Place. About nine. You can talk to the owner. Or his wife. They both saw me."

"Good," she said.

I could see how she was piecing the times together, the chronology, and that it was okay with her, airtight, but then she smiled, a smile that wasn't a cop smile but a woman's smile, and it confused me because there was something about it of the girl next door, that American glance over the fence mixed in there alongside the Chinese. After she was gone I lay there thinking about her, and I thought about Leanora Chinn more that night and about all the boundaries that are never crossed. Whether I contemplated crossing those boundaries, I don't remember, and it wouldn't have mattered anyway because as I lay there the phone rang. It was Marie.

"Micaeli Romano called me today," she said. "His mother's having a birthday this week and he's having a small party. Down in Pescadore. He asked me to come."

"Yeah?"

"And he asked me to ask you."

I hesitated. I remembered how Wong had said Micaeli Romano had work for me—but there was all that tangled family history to contend with, and my brother's dislike of the man, and other things I could not remember. Then I thought of Marie, and of the drive to the coast with her, and I said yes, of course, because it was in my blood to say yes to her, and how could you resist your blood.

TEN
PESCADORE

We drove down to Micaeli's place in Marie's white convertible and thrilled along with the top down, winding through Devil's Slide, the stark hillsides above and below us the plunging ocean. Marie wore sunglasses, her hair tied in a bandanna, and I rode in the passenger seat crouched beneath the wind. I was not sure I wanted to see Romano but I wanted to be with Marie, and when we reached the long stretches of open road below Half Moon Bay, and the sun burned through the fog, it seemed this was what I had been meant to do, ride beside my dead brother's wife in a foreign convertible, whipped about by the heat and the cold.

"Lieutenant Chinn came to your apartment, the day of the funeral?" I asked.

"Yes."

"What did she ask you?"

"Just questions."

"About us?"

"About if I'd seen Joe lately." Marie flashed her hand through her hair, and there was something in the gesture that said she did not want to talk about this anymore. I continued anyway.

"Did she ask about us?"

"It was so long ago, I didn't think it mattered," she said. "Anyway, she already knew."

"From Luisa?"

"I guess."

"Did she ask your whereabouts the night of the murder?"

"Yes."

"What did you say?"

"The truth. Can we talk about something else?"

"Where were you?"

"You too?" she asked. "Are you a cop now too?"

"Just asking."

"All right. I was out to dinner."

"Where?"

"The Flower of Italy."

She didn't have to tell me anymore, or even tell me who she'd been with, because I knew. Or at least I had a pretty good idea. The Flower of Italy was a favorite with the old school Italians, Micaeli Romano in his day—and now Michael Jr.

On the hills above San Gregorio the fog closed in over us, and I could feel again the ocean chill a bit fiercer than I liked, and the sound of the wind whistling past grew louder, isolating Marie and me from one another, too loud to hear one another talk.

Micaeli Romano's farm was off the road south of Pescadore, between the ocean and the highway, an old estate that had been built some hundred years ago in the manner of an Italian villa, ornate trim and high porticos, painted in colors that had long since begun to fade and peel. The house sat in a valley warmer than the surrounding country, where the artichokes grew in long rows and Mexican laborers worked with knives to remove the thistle from the plant. All of it was Romano's land, bought by his father some fifty years before, allowed to degenerate to a kind of European indolence. I had been here once when I was a child, and I knew Marie and my brother had spent some weekends down here, back when they were still married and Joe had wanted the old man to invest in one of his building ventures. I knew too that Marie had returned here after her divorce with Joe, and that's where she'd met up with Michael Jr., though I didn't know if that last part was true or whether the old man had any idea of the rumors that tied Marie to his adopted son.

We pulled into the gravel drive. Some ocean-beaten date palms lined the way, and the pampas grass grew thick and wild all the way to the house. The old man himself came out to meet us, dressed in his baggy pants and his white shirt and his suspenders, clothes he had taken to wearing in his older years, as if now that he were an old man he wanted also to look as if he lived in an earlier century.

"Nick."

He said my name all by itself, as if it were a magic charm, and I saw something like tears in his eyes. He gave me the embrace old Genovesi give to one another—though in fact I am not Genovesi—pulling me close and putting his cheek against mine, once on each side. I felt the old complicated emotions I always felt toward Micaeli and broke away from him as soon as I could. He embraced Marie the same way, only for a little longer; then he stood back to look us both over the way old people like to do. Then, nodding his approval, he led us into the house.

"This place, it was built by Marco Fontana. In a certain tradition," said Micaeli. "There are not so many places like it. Not here. Not in Italy anymore either. It loses me money but I don't care."

We stood on the verandah looking toward the road. Marie was inside, unpacking. Later this afternoon Micaeli's son would arrive and also Micaeli's sister and his brother-in-law, the old man Ernesto Tollini, all coming to celebrate the birthday of Guilia Scarpaci Romano. The matriarch, half-senile, older than anybody wanted to believe.

"Marie's missing this wine. It's awful good," I said.

"She'll be along, don't you worry."

"But it has such a nice taste."

"Pour us some more."

I filled our glasses and drank. The wine came from some old crony of his, a vineyard in the interior, and had about it the taste of those empty hills. The old man watched me drink with pleasure. He was a good-looking man even now. Micaeli was somewhere in his seventies, though until recently he had defied his age, not graying really, staying clear-eyed and limber, lifting his head to laugh and drawing in public the looks of women ten, twenty years younger than himself. He was more gaunt now and seemed to have lost some weight, but his features still haunted you in a pleasant way, and his dark eyes still fixed you when he spoke.

"You know I was always fond of your brother," he said at last. "We had our troubles. I didn't like some of the things he did to Marie. And when his business went dry, you know, he blamed it on me."

"It doesn't matter now."

"It does matter," Micaeli insisted. "You, your brother, your mother, you have always been like family to me. Marie too," he said, nodding his head towards the house. "A man reaches my age, he has regrets. About this thing over here maybe. Or this piece of his past. I think you know some of mine. How it was once, with your mother and me."

"She had a husband, you know. My father." I spoke with some anger. "You didn't need to keep coming around."

"Maybe not. But your mother and I, after the war, after I married Vincenza, it was different between us. Just talk between old friends at the kitchen table. But your father couldn't let go his jealousy."

"Would you?"

"I did. Or I did my best. But you, Nick, you. I know that you've had some trouble and I want you to pull yourself together. Your mother would want this too. Meanwhile there is some help you can do for me."

I took another sip of the wine, waiting to see what was coming. Micaeli smiled and it was that irresistible smile, I remembered it from long ago, and I smiled back, not knowing whether to hate him or to love him; then he reached across and touched me on the arm.

"But no business now. Tomorrow. In the afternoon. We talk in my office."

Marie appeared on the porch and behind her was Vincenza Romano, Micaeli's loyal wife, tall for an Italian woman and regal, wearing a floral print dress and carrying a tray of bread, a saucer of oil. As they stepped onto the verandah, a car pulled into the drive. It was Micaeli's only son, Michael Jr. He drove a new sedan, elegant, European, and he and his wife and his kids were like something out of a picture book, the way they raised their heads and sauntered up the walk. Michael Jr. wore a black suit, he had dark curly hair, and though he had been adopted, you would never know so. He looked more like a Genovesi, an Italian of the North, even than his father.

His wife was an elegant woman, purebred Anglo, thin of bone, sheer blonde hair. I watched her as she came up the stairs to see how she reacted to Marie, but there was nothing there I could see. Either she didn't know about her husband's affair with Marie, or that rumor wasn't true.

"Good to see you, Mike. It's been a long time."

"Too long."

Michael Jr. lowered his voice in the manner of his father and clasped me at the elbow.

"I'm sorry about Joe."

He seemed embarrassed, looking for something else to say but not finding it, and I just shrugged my shoulders. He was ten years younger than me, and I remembered the fuss when Vincenza and Micaeli signed the adoption papers, but the truth was I never really cared for him and maybe resented the life that had been laid out before him.

Michael Jr. walked over to his mother, embracing her in the way his father had embraced me. He did the same to his father, then Marie, and as he did so I watched Michael Jr.'s wife again, the faces of his parents, of Marie, how she closed her eyes when his cheek pressed against hers, but no one seemed to be paying any attention but myself.

"It's wonderful to have the family together," said Micaeli and he put one arm around his son, the other around Marie, and pulled them close at the same time, clutching them to his Italian heart.

We ate dinner in the front room, Micaeli sitting at the head, his wife Vincenza beside him. They placed the old matriarch at the end opposite, where she sat perched in her antique dress, lace collar, eyes glazed with cataracts. Guilia was the birthday girl, ninety-seven years old. She wore a thick layer of porcelain-colored makeup, giving her the look of a broken doll whose face had been plastered with mud. I ended up next to her, while Marie was on the other side of the table, next to the Tollinis. Teresa Tollini was Micaeli's sister, and her husband Ernesto was a restaurateur, a buddy of Micaeli's from the old days. They had brought a couple of their grandkids with them, and these kids sat together with Romano's grandkids at a smaller table in the next room, hands and faces immersed in their spaghetti, the thick sauce, color of blood, that was like a drug once you got started eating and couldn't stop. When I was young I would eat until I was silly, sitting alongside cousins and cousins-of-cousins, all of whom would eat more and more—and eventually I would give up, defeated, because I was only half Italian, after all.

"Ah, Nick," said Ernesto Tollini, leaning across the table. "At least you still live in North Beach. All the other young ones, they have left the neighborhood."

"I guess I'm the only one not to make it rich."

"Good for you, my boy, good for you. There are other things besides money. It is nothing but tourists in my restaurant now."

"It is not just the young ones who left," said Mrs. Tollini. "It's everyone. No one cares nothing about the old neighborhood anymore."

Micaeli's sister had always liked to argue, and the argument Teresa Tollini was launching now had been going on since I was a kid. The Italians should stick close, stay in the neighborhood. It had seemed a vital argument twenty, thirty years before, the cause of much anguish and shouting as neighbor after neighbor loaded their cars, their trucks, and hauled off toward a better life. It seemed beside the point now. Mrs. Tollini brought it up anyway, directing it to her brother Micaeli, who had abandoned them like the rest.

"That's not true. We still have our law office in town. And I walk the streets every day," said Michael Jr. He smiled in that agreeable way he had, the good son following his father's path even though the footsteps in front of him were too large and he wobbled as he went.

"No," said Mrs. Tollini. "You don't walk the streets. You drive the streets. You park beneath the building and when the day is over you drive home to Los Altos. That is not what I call living in the neighborhood. Like your father.

When he's not here, on his farm, he's in that condominium in Sausalito."

"More wine?" asked Vincenza Romano, the good wife. She headed toward Mrs. Tollini with the bottle, her goal to distract the conversation. Mrs. Tollini did not want to be distracted. Meanwhile Marie was talking to Helen Romano, Michael Jr.'s wife, and the two women tilted toward one another, laughing, a gay kind of laughter, and I was sure then that there had been nothing between Marie and Michael Jr. Or almost sure.

"We all make our mistakes," said Ernesto Tollini. He was addressing his old buddy Micaeli. They slipped into Italian as they did whenever they talked of the old days. I caught enough to understand they were discussing Ettore Patrizi, the newspaper editor whose widow Angelica had died in a nursing home just the week before.

"Angelica never got over what they did to her Ettore," said Teresa Tollini. "They had no right."

"Ettore was in love with Mussolini. Every column in his newspaper praised Il Duce, even after the war started. That's why he ended up in jail."

"Those days everyone was in love with Mussolini. Churchill. Gandhi. Before the war, all the great men visited Il Duce's estate in Rome. They were all impressed."

"But they did not stay in love with him. Ettore did not have enough sense to sniff the wind."

"Bah," said Teresa Tollini. *La Italia* was an Italian newspaper. Who was Ettore supposed to write about? He helped bring Marconi to North Beach, remember? And Caruso, all the great Italian artists. The reason the government put him in jail was not because he was a fascist. It was Italian culture he was writing about. And Roosevelt did not want for us to be Italians anymore."

Micaeli slapped his hand on the table and his old judge's voice boomed out.

"Ettore Patrizi *was* a fascist!"

There was a bit of theater in the old man's posture. Then, though, his eyes darted furtively at Marie, and she looked away from him, down at her plate. I did not know the meaning of this exchange, and thought that Marie was thinking about her own father, who had disappeared from North Beach before she was born. (There were rumors about him—an adventurer, an Italian loyalist, a drunk—but then there were rumors about everyone. The truth, Marie told me once, was that he had died during the Korean War. Then, after her mother's death, Marie had been raised by her uncle on her mother's side, and she had taken the uncle's last name.)

The room fell quiet. It had been years since I had heard a conversation like this and then only in whispers. Most of North Beach had been touched by the scandal, even my mother and father, who had been forced to sit before the Tenney Committee in 1942, back when the government was grilling everyone who ever walked through the door of the Italian Social Club.

"Hush, let us be quiet. These are all dead people. It is not worth arguing over them," said Ernesto. "There is no need to go over this one more time. Our grandchildren, please."

The grandchildren, as if on cue, looked up from their spaghetti. I remembered doing the same, hearing the rush and flutter of the adult conversation build to a pitch, then a sudden stop, an insistence on silence. Even so, I'd gathered enough over the years to know the details of what had happened, or what people thought had happened. When the Committee got my mother on the stand, she had refused to talk. My father was a different story. He recited the names of a dozen or more local Italians, doing so, he said, because his wife had fallen into bad company and he did not want her to go to jail. My father was not the only one to cooperate.

One man named as a fascist sympathizer had been Micaeli himself. On the witness stand, though, Micaeli gave such a speech, full of love and patriotic devotion to America, expressing it not just on his own behalf but the behalf of all other Italians, the cannery workers, the net menders, the old women in their black dresses, that the allegations against him did not stand. In the end it was only a handful who went to jail. Even those who did go, what exactly they had done, aside from listen to Mussolini on the radio, no one was really sure.

Teresa Tollini held a grudge and was not ready to let it go. "It's not fair. Look at the Chinese. They walk up and down Grant Street, waving red flags, Mao say this, Mao say that. No one arrests them. Instead, we do business with them, we sell them our neighborhood."

"*Basta!*" shouted Ernesto. "Enough is enough." Ernesto was red in the face and wanted to exert his authority. He turned to me. "I'm sorry to hear of your brother. It is a great unhappiness." He paused, staring into his sauce. A little bit of it stained his chin. "I saw him down in North Beach, you know, a couple of weeks ago. In Portafino's."

This puzzled me. Portafino's was an old man's hangout, full of old Italians playing cards. I looked to Marie again, but she seemed to have disengaged. It was not like her not to be listening, though, and I wondered if she were putting it on.

"Paying his respects. A good man, your brother."

"Yes, I remember your brother, a beautiful boy," said Guilia Scarpaci Romano all of a sudden. All this time the ancient matriarch had been so silent beside me that her voice took me by surprise. Her eyes, glazed as they were, looked at nothing in particular, but her voice, tinny and a bit hoarse, sounded like a melody recorded in an earlier age, though the equipment that played it back was not so good anymore. "And where is your wife, that beautiful woman you married? Anne, that's her name. Your mother always talked so wonderfully about her."

The others at the table glanced down, embarrassed for me. Micaeli's mother went on praising Anne's looks, her sophisticated demeanor, apparently unaware how in the end Anne and I had never married.

"And your mother, you know, she was so proud of you. There wasn't a woman in North Beach more beautiful than your mother. Isn't that true, Micaeli?"

This caused more embarrassment at the table. The old woman had a sly smile on her face and I wondered if maybe she wasn't more aware than she seemed. Meanwhile Vincenza Romano jumped up and brought in the spumoni.

She put it around the table, a slice in front of everyone, and brought a candle for every slice. Then she handed round some matches.

"The reason for all our problems," old Guilia said, "is because us, we Italians, we hate ourselves. In North Beach. And in Italy, it is the same, always. North hates South. Sicilian hates Florentine. Brother hates brother."

"Mama," Micaeli raised his voice as if to silence her, but something had been triggered inside his mother and she would not quiet easily.

Vincenza Romano bent over the old woman and lit her birthday candle.

"That's why that man, that communist, why he shot Il Duce. He was jealous of the old man's mistress and wanted Claratta Petacci for himself. So he shot Mussolini through the heart," Guilia said. Her eyes gleamed in the candle light. "Yes, those were the great days. Before they killed Il Duce. I remember them well."

There was a pause now, everyone regarding old Guilia, who held her head as if she were far away, looking at something else. Her necklace was beautiful about her neck.

"That's right," said Teresa Tollini, but you could tell in her voice she wasn't going to let it go. She had, of course, her own views on the subject. "But if you ask me, it was all the fault of Claratta Petacci. She coddled up to the Germans—and Il Duce went along—all because she wanted to go to the opera in Berlin. That's the truth of it."

"No!" Micaeli's voice was firm again. He'd had enough of his sister's ranting. After all, he had fought in Italy against the fascists and knew the truth of things. "Every time a great man falls, they blame a woman. But sometimes, you have to blame the man himself."

"Bah," said his sister, shooting a sudden, vicious glance at Marie. "Claratta Petacci was a scheming bitch."

ELEVEN
WHITE SAND

The next afternoon Marie and I left the house, going off through the pampas grass to the white dunes. For me, walking through the sand was thick and heavy business. I tried going barefoot, like Marie, but the sand scorched my feet and I was forced to stumble along in my city shoes. The sand did not bother Marie though; she seemed to float along. She wore a pale blouse that hung loose over her shorts. In the gleam of the sun, underneath the blank and shining sky, her hair no longer was blonde but luminous and white.

"How do you take the sand?"

"My feet are callused. From walking on the beach."

"There's no beach in North Beach," I said. It was an old line but it was true. The name had been given before they filled the flats with slag and concrete.

"Maybe so. But there are beaches other places."

We reached the edge of the water, where I could take off my shoes and mince along in the wet sand. I followed behind Marie and watched her, thinking how she had looked as a girl, her thin legs and her dark eyes and her long hair. I could see the same spirit in her now but there was something else too that seemed a betrayal of that spirit, and that betrayal made me ache for her all the more, for both what she was now and what she had been once upon a time.

We were still within sight of the house when Marie turned to me without warning, her face troubled. She said my brother's name.

"Joe."

I stood close to her. I waited for her to say something more, to reveal some memory, some event from their past. Her lips parted but suddenly I did not want to hear his name again. I embraced her, crushed myself against her, and it was a continuation of that other day on Ocean Beach, only with no reserve. My hand loosened the tie on her shorts, they were a gauzy material and opened in front like a sarong, nothing underneath, and I felt her breath against my cheek, and the name she whispered—as I touched her between the legs and she pulled me close—was no longer my brother's but my own. Then we remembered Romano's house behind us and hurried to be out of sight of the long porches that faced the sea. I took her by the hand and we went over to the dunes and lay down between them, and she rolled over onto me, and I put one hand under her pale blouse, onto her breasts, and slid the other into the loose wildness beneath her shorts. The sarong fell open again. She pulled at the opening in my slacks and rolled me on top of her, and we went after each other like that for a long time, until at last we were done, and the shadow of the clouds moved over our bodies, and our breath quieted, and we could hear again the cawing of the gulls and the crashing of the waves.

Now she lay still beneath me. I touched her face. She held the hem of my shirt between her fingers and looked past me at the gulls. I remembered how she had told me, back when I first started up with Anne, how she would get me back one day, she would make it a mission in her life and would not stop until she was done.

"I'm going to go to hell," she said.

"Maybe. But not for this."

"Joe . . . ."

"Joe's dead. Besides you two have been finished for years."

"That's not what I mean. We should be quiet, I think, about what's been happening between us."

"Maybe so. It doesn't look right. Not so soon."

"I don't want Micaeli to know," she said.

"What does it matter, old man Romano, what he knows?"

"He's dying."

"How can that be?"

"Cancer. It's all through him."

"He looks okay."

"But that's not how he is. And there's that Inspector Chinn, you know."

"What about Inspector Chinn?"

"She seems to be looking for somebody to blame."

"You didn't seem worried about her before."

"I'm not worried."

Marie rolled out from under me onto her stomach. She lay there looking away from me, out through the dunes toward the ocean. I wanted to touch her but I resisted. I remembered her dark moods and how she could be, how when she was a kid that darkness was all wrapped up with the father she'd never seen, whom she romanticized one minute and hated the next. So I didn't say anything. Instead I just watched her, studying the length of her body, the cinch of her waist, the reach of her legs and the arch of her foot. The sarong was still half undone, riding higher up her legs now, and it revealed on her thigh something that had been hidden during our lovemaking. A bruise. Just beneath the buttocks, large as the palm of my hand, ugly and mottled at its center. I reached out to touch.

"What's this?"

"I fell down the stairs."

"How long ago?"

"A couple weeks."

"Pretty nasty."

"Not so bad as it looks—and it doesn't hurt much anymore. You should've seen the bump on my head."

"What happened?"

"Stupidity," she said. "I slipped."

She reached back to push my hand away, then pulled the sarong over the bruise, and went back to staring at the sea. I thought of what Chinn had told me, about the argument the neighbors had overheard at Marie's place. I let it go. After awhile she rolled back to me and I felt the warmth of her stomach against mine, and my mouth pressed against hers, and I forgot everything. I told myself there wasn't anything I wouldn't do to keep her next to me like this for-ever. We were like animals that had found each other after years wandering some impossible landscape, and now that we were joined we would tear each other apart rather than be separated. Then she jolted up, headed toward the house, and I followed at a distance, struggling along through the sand.

I lay in my room and listened to Marie in the shower. When she was done, I went in and soaped myself. Even after I had washed clean I felt no one could look at us without knowing what we had done, without smelling it on our skin. So I changed my clothes again and tried to make myself presentable for the old man.

The door to his study stood loose, but Micaeli was not there. I edged in anyway. A wood-paneled room, colors dark and masculine, filled with the stuff of his long career. Leather-bound books and yellowing files, handcrank adding machine and laminated ashtrays. Standing brass lamp, shade like a woman's corset, viper's tail winding up its spine. Pictures of family, diplomas hanging on the wall. Not haphazard but neat and orderly, as his office in North Beach had been. I remembered visiting it when I was a boy. How it had reassured me, the smell of ink and paper, all those books there with the law inside them. And I remembered my mother standing beside me, meek with her love of him, and myself despising her for it, when I was old enough to despise, and despising him too—but at same time I could not help but want to be under Micaeli's wing, to be an insider, loved by this man who was not my hopeless and stupid father. Glancing around I felt the same now. This should be my life to inherit. Not the adopted son's, who'd had his taste of everything, even Marie.

The window overlooked the ocean. I could see down the beach all the way to the lighthouse at Pigeon Point, past the spot where Marie and I had fucked in the dunes. I put myself on tiptoes and placed a hand on the bookcase to get a better look. At my fingertips was a leather valise, like the one Jimmy Wong had given me to deliver down in Chinatown. I noticed it now. I caressed its soft leather just as Micaeli entered the room

"Admiring the view?"

"You can see quite a ways. Down over the dunes."

"There's some binoculars there. Second shelf down. You can see everything with them. Even women on sailboats, out at sea."

"How about people on the beach?"

"Them too."

We bantered back and forth a bit and all the while I kept thinking of myself and Marie out there on the dunes, wondering if anyone had seen us. With each moment it seemed to matter less and less, as if it had happened in some distant time, long ago, perhaps in the same universe where the young bachelor Micaeli Romano wandered the streets of North Beach in love with a married woman. My mother. Before the war and my father's injury. When my brother and I had not yet been born.

"I don't know that you will be interested, but I want to offer you a job."

"Jimmy Wong mentioned something like that."

"I just want you to think about it. You don't have to answer me now."

"What kind of work?"

"You may have heard about the China Basin Project. It's a joint venture—and it will require a team of lawyers in several capacities. I want you to be part of that team."

"To do what?"

"Tenant advocacy."

He said it without a blink. As if he did not know how far I'd fallen or what kind of work I did for Jimmy Wong. I had a hard time believing that, though it was true Micaeli wasn't much in touch anymore, and it was possible he didn't really know, or didn't want to know.

"There'll be some neighborhood groups, you know how the city is these days. Everyone will want their slice. I want you to work with these people, keep them on our side."

It seemed crazy at first, given what I had been doing, but reputation is a funny thing, I knew, easy to twist around this way or that. I had worked both sides of the fence after all, the Chinese and the Italian, and there weren't too many people of any consequence who would step forward and complain.

"I thought you had retired," I said.

"A man like me isn't allowed to retire."

Micaeli said it with Genovesi bravado, a little flourish of his hands, pleased with himself. He puffed out his chest, and it was this type of thing, this vanity and pleasure with himself, that had so irked my brother. "But I'm a figure-head. They don't allow me to work, they just want my name. Still I ask nice, they listen to me. But I don't want to rush you. You think about. There are some men from Hong Kong I will be entertaining. You should meet. But first make an appointment with my son."

"Michael Jr.?"

"He runs the office in North Beach, you know that?"

"Yes."

"Go see him. Now—enough of this. Let's live our lives."

He embraced me and I embraced him back, heartily, not thinking about things that I should, maybe, but instead about some other life that I wanted to have lived.

TWELVE
PORTAFINO'S

At dusk I was back on Broadway. It was a busy Sunday night, lonesome, full of laughter, and the door hawks grabbed the collar of every dollar bill strutting by.

"Come inside," they insisted. "Come wet your noodle, buddy. Come take a naked peek."

"What you got so good for me?"

"We got a feast for the eyes, Mr. Honey Jam. Guaranteed exhilaration. And a napkin to cover your lap."

All over North Beach the lights stung the air with some kind of neon melancholy, and the sidewalks burned with a hundred, a thousand, ten thousand shuffling feet. Marie wasn't with me. It had all unraveled between us on the way home, in the car, when she asked me how it went with Romano.

"I can't take a job with him."

"Why not?"

I didn't answer this because I didn't have an answer. The truth was I wanted the job, but every time I decided yes, I'd do it, a lump came into my throat.

"It's because of your brother, isn't it?"

"I don't know what you mean."

"It's some deal you two made with each other. Maybe you never spoke it out loud but it was a deal anyway. If either of you gets something nice, you throw it away. Just heap it on the trash."

"That's not true."

"But you don't have to pay attention to that deal any-more you know. Your brother's dead. Offer expired."

"Funny girl."

"Or did you sign the contract in perpetuity?"

I let out a harsh little laugh. I wanted to say something nasty. Maybe ask about Michael Jr. and the rumors I'd heard, and just how did she afford that little place of hers up on Telegraph Hill anyway? But I didn't say a thing. Partly it was the look on her face. I took it as sadness first, but the longer we drove the more I studied that face, the way it responded to the shadows of the road as they fell across her features, how her lip trembled at the passing cars and her eyes widened in the narrowing light. Her fingers tightened on the wheel and her knuckles whitened and the conversation between us all but died.

"Sometimes you've got to have the nerve to do something," she said. "When it all closes in, you got to have the nerve. You have to take it in your own hands."

I didn't say anything to this. It sounded like words I'd told myself a time or two, and that led to trouble if I bothered to listen.

When we hit the neighborhood I had her drop me off at the base of the hill. I brushed her lips with mine but the kiss was furtive and cold, and I told myself I had no idea if I had the kind of nerve she meant.

Down Broadway I felt again as if everything between us on the beach had been an interlude. Now I walked the everyday streets, and the distance between us was the same it had always been, just a few blocks, but really much more than that, a kind of perennial twilight in which we circled one another, our hands outstretched but never touching, like the man and the woman whose distraught images were painted in velvet on the walls of the Naked Moon.

My usual evening routine was to hit Mama Mia's first, a little slophouse down Columbus Avenue. Then I'd drink for a while in the A-1 Lounge before heading up to Kim's, then back to the joints on Broadway. I followed the same path almost every night and it made a nice little loop.

Only tonight Mama Mia's spaghetti tasted liked the slop it was, and I had no stomach for all those losers, heads down, forever rolling off their stools inside the A-1. Also I had the notion I was being followed. By vice maybe, or Chinn's people—but I couldn't put the spot on anyone definite. I sauntered past the Montgomery Block, where the bohemians used to slouch and smoke their dope, jerking off in the dirty mattresses, then I headed up past the rubble of the International Hotel. An old beatnik squatted in those stones muttering to himself, reciting the names of poets who would be forgotten in the next century. It was a long list and the names were indecipherable in his throat. Overhead loomed the TransAmerica Pyramid. The domino players in Portsmouth Square, the struggling shopkeeps and vegetable men, they all liked to say how at twilight you can see in the windows the ghosts of all the business men who have died of heart attacks inside. All I have seen though are executives emerging from the underground parking garage, faces serene and inviolate behind the tinted windows of their beautiful cars.

I went over to Kim's earlier than usual and found a different crowd. Something had changed over the weekend. At first I thought it was the hour, or I had walked in the wrong door, but no. New management had taken over and the place had gone pastel. The crowd was young and beautiful and Chinese and smiled at one another in their American clothes. The photographs of the Italians had been taken from the wall. Outside an old Chinamen with no place to drink cursed and spat on the walk.

I contemplated that offer old man Romano had made and felt inside my chest a feeling wild and sad. Meanwhile the white fog cascaded down Kearny and the strains of some prerecorded saxophone wailed in Carol Doda's old joint. I thought of my brother in his grave up in Colma, how all he had really wanted was to be let inside the house, where the sauce was being ladled thick and sweet. It was all I wanted too, I suppose, but I couldn't accept the old man's offer, just as I couldn't walk up the street and knock on Marie's door. Marie was right. I didn't have the nerve. That house might be open for me, but no way could I bring myself to walk inside and sit at the table.

I suppose I could have given myself a little bit of analysis about that. How it came to be that me, the man on the outside, was the eviction agent. And who was it I was trying to punish, when I threw those son of a bitches out on the street? I didn't dwell it over though. Instead, I took my feet further down Columbus. In a little while I found myself with nowhere to go, standing in front of Portafino's. Like everybody else I ignored the joint and would not have given it a second glance if Ernesto Tollini hadn't seen my brother inside a couple weeks before.

Portafino's is dark like a cave, a place with tired walls,

bare and plain, tables with no cloths, no menus, nothing but bottles behind a bar and old men playing cards. Though the door is always open, few outsiders wander in. Anyone can see at a glance it's no one here but the nobodies of Little Italy, talking about the old country, muttering in their mother tongue. Don't matter that the old country is not what you remember and never was, because the mother tongue, she don't care about details so small and precise. Inside Portafino's there wasn't much to see. Just the long yellow-necked bottles of Gugliano. The red bottles of Toscano. A wall of liqueurs like that behind the bar, sweet and nauseating, inside porcelain bottles that had waists like young boys and smelled of women who had splashed on too much perfume. The air rancid, walls the color of cigars that had turned yellow and stale in the sun. I looked over the old men playing cards, but their faces had the look of old trees, ravaged by the ages—and there wasn't anyone I could recognize. I decided not to interrupt the card game but to wait for the bartender who stood above them, watching the cards go round.

After a while he came to me, though not in any particular hurry, and it was clear that another two bucks in the register didn't matter to him either way. He spoke in Italian. *"Private club."*

"Chianti," I said. "A glass of Chianti"

He went on speaking in his own tongue. *"Sorry, but it is not possible for me to serve you a drink, only people who have membership in the Italian club."*

Though I had a pretty good idea what he was saying, I didn't want to be given the stiff, so I played stupid. Or maybe Marie had got to me, and I decided to show some nerve.

"No, no. I want Chianti. A glass of red wine."

Meanwhile the old men at the table kept their noses in their cards, their faces hidden beneath the wide brims of their decaying fedoras.

"I'm looking for my brother," I said and slid Joe's picture once again across the bar.

"How am I supposed to know your brother?"

He spoke English now and his big brown eyes glimmered at me from behind the bar. He'd known the language all the time, of course, but had been playing the same game with me he played with the tourists, just to keep me out of this hair.

"He was in here about a week ago," I said. "A few days before he died."

The man took Joe's picture and studied it more curiously now, his mouth open, his eyes intent. He had on his face that troubled, rapturous look people get when they study the faces of the dead.

"He looks like you."

"Do you remember seeing him?"

"I am not here everyday."

"Ask your friends. Maybe they remember."

The bartender shrugged his shoulders, exaggerating his gestures, and tried to hand the picture back to me. "Please. These are old men, this is their place, do not drag such business into here."

"My mother was Rose Abruzzi. We lived on Vallejo Street. Surely one of these men knew her."

"You from the neighborhood?"

"Yeah."

"I never seen you."

"I never seen you either. Maybe it's the age difference."

"You're not so young," he said.

"Go ask them, will ya?"

The bartender relented and took the picture to the old men. They were stubborn and did not want to look up from their cards, but eventually they did, making a big deal about it, leaning back in their chairs and passing the picture around. I could hear my mother's name muttered about the table, and my father's. At length one of the old men came over to me. His face was as old as the fucking wars.

"You do not recognize me. But I recognize you. The instant you walk in this place, I recognize you."

I peered into the old man's face but all I could see was his age.

"I knew your mother, your father, I knew all these men on all these streets. Now you young people, you know nothing."

77

"I agree. It's a sin, the way we are."

"No. Sin is for people who know God. No God, no sin. And life is meaningless without sin."

"I'll commit one soon," I said. "Tell me your name."

"I am no one. Only Sammy Lucca the butcher. I sold your mother meat for twenty years. And I watched you and your brother steal hot dogs from my shelf."

I nodded and peered into his face.

"I remember now," I said, but it was a lie. I didn't remember Sammy Lucca or his hot dogs.

"I knew you would."

"Have you seen my brother around this place?"

"A couple weeks back, he was sitting over at a table here, with John Bruno. You know Johnny? *Il Buffone? Il Facsisto?*" The old man smiled a sad smile. Johnny Bruno, with his Black Shirt still hanging in the closet, was a joke around Little Italy.

"*Si,*" I said.

"Your brother was talking to Johnny Bruno. The two of them left together, went to Johnny's place. Now I want you to pay me for those hot dogs."

I laughed, thinking it was a joke, but Sammy Lucca didn't see anything funny. His friends were watching him from the table, he had his hand out, and it was all a matter of honor now. I'd seen it a hundred million times before. So I gave the old bastard his nickel, plus thirty years interest, then went out to hunt up Johnny Bruno.

THIRTEEN
IL FASCISTO

Johnny Bruno was one of those exiled men Mrs. Tollini had been going on about the other day. One of those San Francisco Italians who had been snatched up and penned inside the Western States Internment Camp during the war. When those men came back to San Francisco, most did not stay long. The streets were wrapped in all that euphoria, confetti tumbling down, and the shame was too much for the *Il Buffone* who had supported Mussolini once upon a time. Shame and then shame again, because how else could it be, all North Beach celebrating and then these men, aliens now, walking about with their heads hanging in everyone else's hoopla. Most gathered their families and scattered soon as they could, and a number ended out in Reno. Johnny Bruno was one of those. He had returned to North Beach after his wife died. His son lived over in Oakland, and this way Johnny could take the subway under the bay once a week and get a look at his grandkids growing up underneath all those eucalyptus trees.

I already knew most of his story but Johnny told it to me again, sitting in his room at the Ling Wei Hotel. The Ling Wei was a pensioners' hotel, formerly the Hotel Colombo, one of the few places around not owned by Jimmy Wong, but that didn't make it any more pleasant. Johnny Bruno sat slumped in a chair under the window, smoking one Pall Mall after another, stinking out the place.

"I read about your brother in the paper. Terrible, the way they kill him."

"Yeah."

"But no one pays any attention these days."

"No."

"Meanwhile, Molini, two hundred years old, he gets an obituary the size of the moon. But what do you expect?"

"I don't know."

"A Genovesi like him, big shot delicatessen owner, he buys himself flowers in advance, pays the newspaper.

Goddamn Genovesi think they can buy everything. When I was a kid, we Sicilians . . . ."

He would've gone on it with, I know, but the Pall Mall got to him and he started to choke. The people in the Mission might lock you out, tell you nothing at all, but these Italians loved nothing better than to intertwine you in their familial wars, so that any slight had precedent in a feud generations old and ultimately pertained to their own grievances more than your own.

"Why did my brother come to visit you?"

"We just talk, that's all."

"What about?"

"The old days, he let me reminisce. But my reminisce, you know, is no sweet stuff. I have some stories to tell and nobody wants to listen. Your brother, I guess, he had his own reasons. But I have my life in boxes all around me. It's the way I am."

It was true. Johnny Bruno's apartment was a cluttered mess, pictures everywhere, Sicilian fishermen, haggard women, Johnny as a young man hanging out in Washington Square, slouching around, curly-headed, arm hanging over some girl's shoulder. He wore his Black Shirt and a cigarette hung from his lips.

"That's what gets me in trouble. I joined the Fascio Umbrile. We met every week. The truth is, some people did not want me in. A Sicilian. But the group, it was paid for by the Italian Consul. And the Consul says everybody gets in. That's the word from Rome. From Il Duce.

"Some people say why you keep this picture in your house? You were no fascist. You were just a young man, you didn't know what the words mean. I say, I have nothing to be ashame."

He stopped here to catch his breath. He wheezed and coughed a little, then pointed at me with his cigarette.

"Your father, they called him to the stand. 1942. Mr. Snitch, he told the USA a list of names. Supposed fascists."

"He wanted to protect my mother."

"No. He did it because your mother was in love with that son of a bitch Micaeli Romano. Your father wanted to punish all the Italians at Fugazi Hall. But I don't blame him, no. The Committee knew his weakness, they had him by the balls."

I was getting tired of Johnny Bruno. He'd a sly look on his face, a bitter old man up to no good in the world.

"Is that what you talked about with my brother?"

"A little bit."

"That all?"

"I'm telling you now. Everything. There were rumors you know, when you were born . . . ."

"The rumors are wrong."

I knew what was coming and cut him off hard. I had heard this story before, when I was about sixteen years old. I didn't believe it then and didn't believe it now, but I had computed out the years once, adding them up in my head to see if it were possible Micaeli Romano was my father. It wasn't. I had been born after the war, my brother two years after that, and all this while Micaeli had still been overseas, serving on the American mop-up crews in Italy. Anyway I had my father's short nose, his Anglo eyes, his Irish feet. I do not look anything like Micaeli.

"The day the Japs hit Pearl Harbor, all that smoke was coming out the radio, so the police buzzed North Beach. They rounded us up. Took us to Sharp Park, we could see the Japs and the Germans the other side of the chain fence. Six weeks before there's even a hearing. But Micaeli, they let him out in two days. His father's money.

"Papa Romano, he was the biggest fascist of them all. Visited Italy and kissed Il Duce's ring. So we were glad when his son, young Micaeli, the lawyer, gets himself sprung. We figure it won't be long before he springs us too."

"Papa Romano renounced fascism. Micaeli . . . ."

"It was a lie. We got messages all the time in jail. 'Romano is still with you. Long live Il Duce!' This kind of shit. Only Micaeli never helped us. He was playing it both ways. Just seeing how the war would go."

This story too was one I'd heard before and so had my brother. It was a story Johnny Bruno had been telling for years, to anyone who would listen, and I was put out with myself for taking the bait. I didn't want to listen anymore.

"I am not finished. You want I should pour you a little wine?"

"I have to go, Johnny."

"Drink the wine, humor an old man. Maybe I tell you something you don't already know."

Johnny Bruno covered a cough and poured the wine. A gleam of triumph, small and mean, emerged in his eyes. He didn't get to tell his story much anymore, but he knew he had me, because I wanted to hear everything my brother had heard.

"It was 1953. Everybody had forgotten the war, but then Luci Pavrotti comes to town. You know, Pavrotti, Mussolini's general?"

I didn't know but Johnny Bruno explained. General Pavrotti had been in the catacombs the day of the Rome Massacre, when 350 Italians were rounded up by the Nazis. The way Johnny Bruno told the story, Pavrotti had been tricked into helping with the roundup, but when he discovered the Nazi's intentions, he stepped in front of their bayonets. "The Germans dare not fire," said Bruno, "Pavrotti was Il Duce's favorite general." A meeting was held, a compromise reached. What was repulsive to the Italians in the catacombs was not to die, but to die at the hands of the Germans. So the women were set free, and the Italian men lined up to be killed at the hands of Pavrotti.

"Kill me now," each man said in turn (or so claimed Johnny Bruno). "I will die for Il Duce," and Pavrotti shot them, one by one, weeping as he walked down the line.

"The Italian communists, the Americans, they twist the story of Pavrotti's heroism. Because the greedy pigs, they want Italy for themselves. So Pavrotti had to run. North Africa, Argentina, Brazil, every dump in the world. Eventually he ends up in North Beach, Columbus Avenue, on his knees in front of Micaeli Romano. Pavrotti is underground in America, broke and busted I tell you, so Micaeli gives him a few nickels and sends him to Reno. But Micaeli Romano was two-faced as ever. Here, I show you what I mean."

Johnny Bruno stood up, his chest thrust forward. He was breathing more easily now, as if telling the story had rejuvenated him. He jerked opened a dresser drawer, shuffling through some papers, but his fingers were not much good anymore, and while he shuffled I peered over his shoulder at a news photo of Mussolini with his mistress, Claratta Petacci. Claratta had on her fur coat, Benito strutted smugly beside her, and when I looked at the two of them like that, I could not help but think of the mob that would desecrate their bodies, passing them hand-over-hand through the crowd, inserting their fingers into the wounds, peeling back the flap of Claratta's skirt. There was something in the slope of their bodies that forecast their future, I thought, that suggested Claratta knew her fate, and for this horrible devotion there was part of me that could not help but loving Claratta, too, at the same time as wanting again to see that picture of her devastated by the mob.

"Here," said Johnny Bruno.

He handed me a scrap of yellow newsprint dated March 15, 1953.

WAR CRIMINAL FOUND DEAD IN HOTEL

Underneath the headline Pavrotti lay dead in a black and white photo, his feet skewed at a crazy angle. The news article told a different version of what happened in the catacombs: how Pavrotti had pulled the gun to show his loyalty to the Germans, then gone down the line, shooting the Italian men as their wives and children watched. He had also been good buddies with Himmler, it turned out, and helped with the execution of Italian Jews. It was clear from the article that officialdom did not much regret Pavrotti's death, and a thorough investigation was nobody's priority.

The article did mention that a man from North Beach had been held in connection with the investigation, then released. The man's name was Dios. I thought about it for a little while, but the name meant nothing to me.

"It was Romano arranged Pavrotti to be killed. He was afraid the public would find out about his own fascist background. He is no good Romano, a traitor to everyone."

"How did Romano arrange it? Through J. Ferrari?"

I was only half-serious, saying it to mock the whole

story, but the old man shook his head and let out a knowing little laugh, as if amused by my naiveté.

"You mean that little monkey man? Down on Broadway. Only old woman go to him. To kill their fat husbands. These days, Ferrari's, it is all tied up with the Chinese. But even then, before the monkey man, no one goes to that place to kill someone important. It is local business only."

"Then how did Romano arrange it?"

Johnny shook his head again, still smiling, but he didn't answer me, and my guess was that he didn't have an answer.

"Did you tell my brother about Pavrotti and Romano? Did you show him this clipping?"

"I can prove what happened. You talk to a man I know. Bill Ciprione. At the Alta Hotel in Reno. He has been quiet almost thirty-five years, but he is tired of the quiet."

"Did you tell my brother about this?" I asked again.

"Sure, I tell him. He wanted a copy of the article, so I walked with him down to Zirpoli's, to the copy machine. Then your brother went to Reno to find the truth for himself. That's why he's dead."

"This guy Ciprione, does he have a phone number?"

"No. Like me, he lives in an old man's hotel. They give us no phone, no refrigerators, no nothing. I don't know how we live, us old men. So you want to talk, you have to go knock on his door."

"Write down his address for me and spell out the name."

"Ciprione, like I told you. He didn't change his name to sound American. Not like a lot of people I know."

"Here, Johnny, on this piece of paper. Write his name and address."

"All of the Italians, they change their name. Susan Hayward. Tony Curtis. Tony Bennet. They were all Italians."

"I know."

"Marilyn Monroe, Joe DiMaggio, all of them, they try to be somebody they weren't. They want to be Smith, they want to be Johnson. It's because we were Italians, you know, that's why they treat us bad. But before the war, everyone was fascist. Henry Ford, Franklin Roosevelt. They kissed Mussolini's feet."

"I remember."

"And now look at you, a Jones. That's all we got left. I been to Italy, and it's the same thing. Pakistanis selling cappuccinos. There's not a goddamn Italian left in the world."

"Okay, Johnny," I said.

He'd finished with the address and I took it away from him. I was tired of Johnny Bruno. I wanted to give him a push, maybe knock him on the floor, but instead I patted his shoulder. This set off a coughing fit and he hacked away like he was being paid to do it.

I used the opportunity to lift the clipping about Pavrotti. If my brother had had a copy, I wanted one too. Then I patted Bruno again and hurried out of the Ling Wei Hotel, passing first through the lobby, under the portrait of Chiang Kai-shek, then out into the street.

On the way home I walked past the Portafino and caught a glimpse of Sammy Lucca inside playing cards. He was passing chips across the table and in that gesture, finally, I recognized him, the butcher from Molini's deli handing change over a counter, and I remembered too my brother and I grabbing the dogs from the butcher case, then running helter skelter into the Italian streets, where the piazzas were gushing water and the fruit was ripe as the Mediterranean sun, and the waters at the end of the peninsula were mysterious and deep and there was no other world but the sweetest of our imagination.

FOURTEEN
REMEMBRANCES

When I was a young man in law school, there was a professor, an old German, teacher of the history of law, who had on his office door a saying from the philosopher Santayana. Something to the effect that those who did not remember history were condemned to fulfill it. I was a diligent boy then, and so I studied my books and read my history and scorned those who led the unexamined life. My own conclusions in years since is that the philosopher may have glimpsed the truth, but he didn't get the whole picture in his eye. Because awareness may let you see what is about to happen, even contemplate its design, but as to whether it opens an avenue of escape, that is another question. It could be recognition is just the last stage in the completion of the design, a trembling of the web, whereby the spider senses exactly where it is we lie.

When my mother died, I discovered in her trunk two stacks of old letters. The first, tied with lavender ribbon, written in Italian and sprinkled with endearments *(Oh bella! Oh mi amore!)* had been sent to her by Micaeli Romano during the war. My command of Italian is not wonderful but I learned from those letters that Micaeli had hoped my mother would defy convention and divorce my father. Those hopes were crushed when my father was injured in a shipboard accident. My mother could not bring herself to leave her maimed husband.

The second stack of letters was unbound, written in the blunt hand of my father.

"Offshore, Corsica. Mussolini on his last legs. Only fifty miles out but all I see is water, flat and endless. German planes yesterday."

My father returned not long after that letter. Micaeli, stationed in Italy, stayed until the end of the war, then signed up for a second tour. He did not come home to North Beach until three years later, until after he had met Vincenza in Florence and married her on the steps of some cathedral.

I first read those letters a few days after my mother was

buried. It was in the old house, and my father was downstairs that day. He'd be dead too, in a few months, but I didn't know that then. I'd been living my life pretty much as they both had wanted, working for a law firm downtown, still engaged to Anne. The longer we were together, the more everyone expected we would be married. I had to admit I liked being with Anne. I enjoyed her wholesome and fervent spirit, and maybe it was true I loved her and was just too stupid to know. Still, I could see our path together snaking ahead through the years. Though that way seemed pleasant and lush, I could not help looking back with a certain longing, especially on those days when I visited Joe and brushed past Marie in the hall. She would glance up at me with those eyes from our childhood, and I'd imagine her warm breath on my cheek and her voice saying she would never let me go, not really, she would be a figure in my dreams, half-buried in the sand, and one day it would be she and I again, embracing in the waves. Or that's the kind of thing that went through my mind when I read those letters.

I was in the middle of them, when my father came into the room. I could see from the way he looked at me that he knew what they were, and maybe he'd read them himself.

"Do you want to me burn these?" I asked.

"No."

"Why not?"

"If I had wanted that, I would have done it a long time ago. Those meant something to your mother."

He always effaced himself; he always acted the fool. "What about you?" I asked. "What do they mean to you?"

My tone of voice, he should've hit me with his crutch; but he didn't. He was long past that. "When you want something," he said, "you have to be cautious."

I laughed.

"Sometimes you have to take your hands off. You chase something too hard, you run it down, you corner it—then you end up killing it. You destroy everything. So instead you let things be. You appreciate something for what it is. Otherwise you are tempting fate. You are looking for trouble. You will start things going you can't control."

"I don't buy it," I said.

"You will. You'll learn to accept things the way they are. So put the letters down."

I put them down, but I didn't agree with him. I did not want to live my life like my father. Nor did I want to do what Micaeli and my mother had done, hiding their desire in letters bound with lavender ribbon. So a few days later I drove down to Redwood City, where Marie and Joe lived as husband and wife in a pretty little bungalow a few blocks from the freeway. I told myself I was going to visit my brother, but of course I knew he worked during the day and it was Marie who answered the door.

We walked together up some naked hillside, Marie and I, making a path through the dry grass. We didn't speak much, because there wasn't much to say. We both knew what was in our heads. Then we reached the top of the hill and sat down under a live oak whose branches looked like an old man's fingers that had somehow sprouted leaves. I put my arms around Marie and we lay beside each other, trembling on that golden hill.

"Let's just hold each other," I said.

"Yes."

"We don't need to do anything else."

"We shouldn't."

"It would ruin everything."

So we lay like that for a little while, like schoolkids touching one another while pretending not to touch. Her dress was thin and the scent of her body under the sun was like the scent of the sky and the earth, and I could not help but caress her, my hand under her billowing dress. Soon her legs wrapped up around my chest and we became fierce like animals under that tree. We did not get off the hill until after four in the afternoon. By then my brother was home. Or at least his truck was in front of his house. So I left Marie off around the corner and drove back to San Francisco.

Six months later they were divorced, and Marie and I met secretly. We met during the day, when I was supposed to be at work; at night, when I was supposed to be in the library preparing a case; on weekends, when I told Anne I was tied up with colleagues. We met in hotels, in diners, in barrooms. We did, I guess, what Micaeli and my mother had done before us. Anne figured it out, but I didn't care. And I didn't care either when I lost my job for not being around. Then, after everything had been risked and the affair could not remain a secret much longer, I plunged my dick into a bucket of ice.

"I can't do this to my brother," I told her.

"You're not doing it to him."

"I can't face him if he finds out."

"What about me?"

"You'll find someone. You're that kind of girl."

"You shouldn't talk to me like that."

"How else should I talk?"

"Like you talked on the hill. With your hand up my skirt."

"I keep seeing his face."

"It didn't bother you before. Just who did you imagine you were fucking?"

"What do you mean?"

"Figure it out."

We fought then, the kind of fight where all the angles of the world are in the wrong places, so that it felt like anything could happen. The next weekend she went to Micaeli Romano's place in Pescadore. She'd been invited there along with her uncle, an old Genovesi like Micaeli, another buddy from the old days. Michael Jr. was there too that weekend. Maybe there was nothing to the stories I heard later, or maybe Marie took up with him to make me jealous, but either way we didn't see each other much after that.

But at least I was a faithful brother. I listened to my father. I let loose of Marie and then Anne and made my life like a mirror, following Joe on his big spiral down.

And now here, at the bottom of the spiral, was Johnny Bruno saying my brother's death, like my father's misery—and the death of Il Duce's favorite general—this too was the fault of Micaeli Romano. I didn't know whether or not to believe him. Maybe I wanted to see how close to the bottom of that spiral I could get. Or maybe there was a part of me that still thought you could make something different out of your future by studying the past. Either way, I decided to take the cash money Jimmy Wong had paid me for delivering his valise, then fly out to Reno and see what I could see.

FIFTEEN
RENO

I caught the next red-eye out, flying alongside a bunch of nervous Neds and Nellies who wanted nothing more than to spend Saturday morning stuffing slots. At the airport I rented myself a car and drove the hazy blue streets, finally settling on a two-story motel called the Big Lucky. My room smelled of gin but at least the Big Lucky was close to the center of town and not so shabby as it might have been. I plugged the machine in the lobby for a while, then hiked over to the Alta Hotel. The Alta was not so very different from the Ling Wei, except it was Teddy Roosevelt's picture in the lobby, and the old bastards who lived here wore string ties on their shirts. They had faces like Indians, those old men, spider crevices under the eyes, skin like leather cured in an atomic wind. The desk clerk wore a cowboy hat. The owners had him jeweled up behind a glass case, bulletproof.

"Bill Ciprione? No such man livin' this here hotel." The clerk ran his finger down the register one name at a time.

"You sure?"

"Not since I had this post."

"How long's that?"

"Three weeks."

"Who's been here longer?"

"Can't truly say. But there's an old son of a bitch for you. Elmore Torn. The one with the gray fedora. Doesn't look like he's been out of the corral as of late."

I hunched beside Elmore. He had fine gray hair and eyes that were very large and blue. I asked him if he knew Bill Ciprione.

"Italian man?"

"Yeah."

"There's a few Italian men here. More before. Which one was he?"

"I'm not sure. Only that his name is Bill. Maybe Billy."

"It's not so smart to get involved with Italians."

"You want a cigarette?"

"Don't smoke."

"Want me to buy you a drink?"

"Too far to walk. Bring one here for me."

"Where do I get one?"

"Down the block. Ernie's Liquors. A can of malt."

"You're too old for malt."

"Get it for me anyway. And I want a cigar."

"I thought you didn't smoke."

"Not cigarettes. Cigars, all right. With a can of malt."

"Okay. I'll go get it for you in a minute. But do you know Ciprione? He's seventy-five, maybe eighty years old."

"The one with the mustache?"

"If you say so."

"Well there was a Bill here, Italian guy, he lived upstairs. 7-A. A couple times, I remember, his daughter came to visit."

"The daughter, she from around here?"

"I don't know anything about her. All I know is the old man used to go every Monday to play cards with his friends. Down at the Ace, you like to talk to his friends. They know more than me."

"Where?"

"The Ace Card Room, that's what I said."

"That's where he is?"

"No. He's dead, sonny. Your friend is dead. Somebody killed him, but he looked like hell anyway. Ugly fuckin' Sicilian."

"He's dead?"

"Yeah. Strangled to death in his room."

"Who did it?"

"Who kills old Italian men? You tell me. I never did understand those people. He didn't have fifteen cents in that room."

The old man touched his hat, which looked older than the dirt itself, and a little piece of the brim came off in his hand. I asked him for directions to the Ace and he told me it was just a few blocks down. He called after me.

"My malt . . . ."

"Don't worry. I'll be back."

I found Ciprione's friends at the Ace, like the old man said. The place was dark inside, like Portafino's, and the men sat regarding their cards just like the old men in North Beach, so I felt as if I had come all this way to talk to these men I had always known but who still regarded me as an outsider. It was the same deal as always. Though they were old and their lives were almost over, I was envious of them. At least in their old age they could dodder off into the sunset, old Italians together. They could stagger up and down the sizzling streets of this disappointed land and tell stories of how things used to be. They did not even look askance as I approached, but I had a sense of mission now and was past being polite.

I slapped the picture of my brother into the middle of their playing table.

"What you want?"

"That picture, it's my brother. He came up a couple of weeks back to a visit a friend of yours. Bill Ciprione."

"Bill's dead."

"So's my brother. I don't think it's coincidence."

The old men just stared. They wanted to go back to their poker. After a while one of them spoke, bald, nodding his head up and down. He was a million years old and had a face like Julius Caesar.

"Ciprione was an old man. Old men, we die. Sometimes young men die too . . . ."

I told him to shut it up. He had that look in his eyes. As if getting ready to go off on one of those speeches old Italians specialize in. Shrugging their shoulders and patting you on the head. In the end telling you nothing, holding all the secrets of the world for themselves.

"You know a man named Micaeli Romano? From North Beach?"

No one spoke.

I could not stand how they denied everything, these old men. I felt the outrage my father must have felt sitting in the witness chair in 1942, knowing how they were all intertwined. The Italians had stolen his wife away, ruined his life, seducing her in the back room of Fugazi Hall, underneath the picture of Il Duce. Yet they just sat there watching him, their eyes sad and innocent, shaking their heads at the way he betrayed them.

"In 1953 Romano arranged the death of Luci Pavrotti. Ciprione knew the details, and my brother came here to talk to him about it. That's why my brother is dead, goddamn it, and that's why Ciprione's dead too. It's not some goddamn coincidence."

One of the old men trembled all over.

"Fuck you," he said to me. "You stupid little boy. Italians, we fought for this country."

"Take it easy," said another one. He gestured at his trembling friend, as if to reprove me. "Fred here discovered the body. They were best friends. Thirty years in business. Foundation work. Bill Ciprione was a good man."

"My brother was a good man too," I said, even though it occurred to me there was room for doubt, same as with anyone. Then for no reason I could put my finger on, I thought of something else. How Chinn had asked about Marie and Joe, if it had ever been violent between them. Though I didn't say anything about it to her, I knew it had been, that in the days before the divorce he'd left his marks on Marie, swatting her up and down the bungalow. I had kept it from Chinn then, and I didn't want to think about it now either. I pushed it from my head.

"I want to get underneath this," I told the old men. "What about his daughter. Where can I find her?"

"Which daughter?" said another one of them, at the far end of the table. His friends gave him a look, as if he were talking too much. The talker turned his head, avoiding my eyes, and I lost my chance to pin him down.

"You're wrong about everything," said Fred. He was in the grips of some kind of palsy now, shaking like a leaf, but it did not affect his speech. "Ciprione died a natural death."

"I heard he was strangled."

"No. He had asthma. He choked in his sleep."

"But the old man—in the gray fedora—he told me . . . ."

"Elmore, he likes a story. Buy him a can of malt, he'll tell you anything."

"Check the newspapers," said the bald one, like Caesar. He glared at me steady, his voice stern, full of authority.

"Look at the medical records. Go to the police. He was just an old man who died in his sleep."

Then the old Italians went back to their cards and I realized they had done with me. They weren't going to talk to me anymore.

On the way back I walked past Ernie's Liquors and strolled inside. I bought the can of malt and the cigar but I didn't take them to Elmore Torn. I walked instead to a park across from one of the casinos, and I opened the can of malt and drank it myself. I knew tomorrow I would do like the old Italians said. I would check the papers, the medical records, the police reports. I would verify the date of death and the cause. Then maybe I would wander around for a while with my brother's picture, check the hotels, but I would find nothing, and I would have no choice but believe the old Italians were telling the truth. Johnny Bruno had sent me on a chase to nowhere.

I finished up the beer and crushed out the cigar, choking a little on the smoke. Then I went back to my hotel room and called Marie. I told her I was out of town on business, but I would be back soon. I told her I wanted to see her. We whispered to each other in hushed tones on the telephone, and I forgot the old men, and I forgot my brother's death, and I told her I would be back the next day, and when just a little time had passed, not too long at all, I'd walk her down Columbus in full view of the world.

But I didn't go back the next day. Instead I checked all the things I knew I should check, talked to all the people to whom I knew I should talk, and they all told me Ciprione had died innocently enough, just like his friends said. Then I got another idea. I leafed my way through the Reno phone book, running my fingers down the long columns of tiny print.

Ciprione, Ellen.

The dead man's daughter. If Joe had been to town last week—if any of Bruno's story was true—then maybe Joe had found his way to the daughter too. It was the only thing I hadn't checked out.

Her address was there in the book, beside the name, and I went there that morning. Her house was about a mile from my motel, a small house on a street of small houses, all built just after the war without too much time or attention. The houses weren't wearing too well, and when Ellen Ciprione came to the door, it didn't look like she was wearing too well either. She was a brunette, a few years younger than myself, with a lot of damage around the eyes. She had that vaguely familiar look such people sometimes have, like maybe she lived in the neighborhood and I passed her on the street every third or fourth day. It wasn't true, though; I had never seen her before.

"Yes?" She regarded me warily.

"My name's Nick Jones," I told her. "I'm coming here because my brother, he was up here about two weeks back. Looking for your father. And I was wondering . . . ."

"My father's dead," she said.

"I'm sorry." I bowed my head a little, as sincerely as I could, but it didn't seem to effect her much. She looked like she'd seen a million guys like me, everyone with a routine, and it was too early in the morning to play along. "Did my brother come here looking for him?"

"Are you a cop?"

"No."

"Then what's your game?"

"I'm trying to find out if my brother spoke to you. Concerning your father?"

"Don't you sons of bitches ever let up?"

I paused a second, taking this in. "Has someone else been here?"

"Just get the hell out. Let the old bastard rest in peace."

She pulled away as if to go inside. I reached out and grabbed her by the arm.

"Let me go."

Her voice was very calm and flat, like she was used to saying this kind of thing to men, telling them to get lost. Up close, I could smell the liquor on her breath and cigarettes. I didn't let go.

"Do you have a sister?" I asked, remembering the old man at the table and what he had implied, and how the others had tried to hush him down. "Maybe my brother talked to her?"

"A sister?"

"Yes, a sister. Do you have one?"

"Let's put it this way," she said. "I'm the only daughter who changed his stinking pants when he was an old man, I was the only one staring into his grave when he died. I am the one and only child of Mr. and Mrs. Ciprione, both deceased. Their vast estate is all mine. Now let me go. And get out of here. Or I start screaming bloody murder."

"Okay, honey," I said. I let her go.

"Don't you honey me," she said.

I thought she would slam the door but instead she stayed on the porch watching me, hands on her hips, as I made my way down the walk. She was still standing like that when I cranked up the engine and drove away.

I had meant to go home that afternoon, back to San Francisco, but I didn't. I didn't call Marie either. Instead, I poked around a few days more, trying to prove the old men liars, and wondering about Ellen Ciprione. I phoned her house again, but she didn't answer. And when I drove by her house, I didn't have it in me to go up and knock. I couldn't see how things would be any different a second time around.

My last night in town I took what I had left of the valise money and moved into one of the large casinos, with the big tables and the free drinks. I felt a little wild, and reckless, and deep inside I felt a pleasure, maybe, that the trip had yielded nothing at all. So I started plugging machines and playing the tables, and I stuck around until I had gambled away all the cash I'd brought with me and half of my account back home. Then I went back to North Beach but I still didn't call Marie. I wasn't ready, not yet. Instead I helped Jimmy Wong with an eviction. He needed some Russian refugees tossed out of a place in the Sunset District. I ended up standing in their door with my arms crossed like a Cossack, while Rickie and Eddie Lee carried their junk out into the street. Their name was Rudski, and later I read in the paper how Mr. Rudski had gotten drunk and hung himself with a lamp cord in a Tenderloin hotel. Only the cord had stretched and Rudski wound up in San Francisco General with a burn the size of Nebraska around his neck.

"Don't feel bad," Jimmy Wong told me later. "It's not your fault. Ever since Stalin died, these Russians, they don't know what they're doing. They're ignorant fools. Dumber than shit. They need someone to tell them what to do."

SIXTEEN
SHOES IN THE CLOSET

"Where have you been?"

"Inside."

"Your apartment?"

"The bottle."

"That isn't funny."

"It wasn't meant that way."

"I talked to Micaeli. He said you were going to meet with his son this week."

"That's what I told him in Pescadore."

"He just means you the best, you know."

"I know," I said. "I want to see you."

Marie fell silent. Though we were just a few blocks away, our connection was poor and I could hear chatter on the wire. A man and woman speaking back and forth, yes, no, then both at once, unrestrained, laughing. Their voices were happy, innocent, as ours might be, if we lived on the other side, beyond the pale. Then the connection sharpened and the silence was pure.

"How about tomorrow evening," Marie said at last. "Around eight."

"I'll be there."

Since returning from Reno, I'd had time to think things over and then think them over again. Maybe my brother believed he had something concrete against Romano, but it seemed he was wrong. The only loose wheel, maybe, was Ellen Ciprione. From this distance, though, she didn't amount to much, just a slatternly woman, half-drunk, living by herself in a desert far away. So it seemed there was nothing to Johnny Bruno's story. Even if there was, it all happened too long ago to matter any more. Rather, the truth was what it appeared to be. Bill Ciprione had died an old man's death in an old man's hotel. And my brother had died because he'd been standing on the wrong street corner at the wrong time of night with the wrong look on his face. No, Romano was clean, like the snow was clean before it hit the ground. This was what I told myself now. I was free to do as I pleased.

*   *   *

Marie's building was ordinary enough on the outside. Stucco walls, white trim, a doorway edged with glass blocks. Inside her place had more glitz. The walks and tiles had been redone not so long ago, and a pair of glass doors looked out to where the steamers came into the bay. On the other side of her apartment a deck came off the kitchen and a set of stairs led down to Telegraph Gardens, an old grove full of palms and bougainvillea and wild flowers, all tumbling into a canyon at the edge of Telegraph Hill. When we were kids it had been a ragged place hung with laundry and frequented by old drunks. Now the gardens were tended and the old Victorians along here—brightly painted with elaborate cornices—these houses were worth plenty. I wondered again how Marie got her money. Maybe she had inherited a little bit when her uncle died, but it couldn't have been enough to keep her going long, not here.

"Nice place."

"It is."

"You got this in the settlement?"

"Don't be silly. Joe didn't have anything. And if it were mine, I'd sell it fast."

"Where would you go?"

"Away from North Beach."

"You've had plenty of chances for that. Why haven't you gone already?"

"You should know the answer."

We lingered in the darkened parlor. A car crawled up the hill outside, and its lights shone up through the slanted blinds, casting a shadow on Marie's face. The light was like a cold hand touching her cheek. She closed her eyes and her lips trembled and I could see the distress in the crooked turn of her neck.

"You upset about Joe?"

"You didn't really know your brother."

"I think I knew him pretty well."

"Before he died he started coming up here."

"What did he want?"

"To talk. And the way your brother talks, people see

100

him, they think he's goddamn Christopher Columbus, that swagger. But you get him alone everyone's responsible for his problems but himself."

"What did he say?"

"He wouldn't leave me alone. He was obsessed."

"With you?" I asked.

She brushed her hair away with her hand, pulling it back, and I could see the dark roots underneath the blonde. "Let's not talk about this anymore. Pour us some wine."

"Just a minute."

We still stood in the parlor and I wanted to kiss Marie there, in the spot where the light had poured through the blinds. She resisted but I put a hand on each shoulder and pulled her near. Then she kissed me hard, a kiss that was angry and cold. Our bodies touched, leaning into one another below the waist, but we did not embrace. Marie yanked her head back and I saw the cold flash in her eyes, and she must've seen something in mine too because we both looked away as if frightened by what had just risen between us. Anything could happen, I realized. I was capable of anything. And so was she.

"There's a sauce on the stove," she said. "It needs stirring."

So I poured the wine and Marie set the table and together we brought out the food. It made for a nice scene at the table, domestic and pretty, and we both smiled and acted at ease, ignoring that moment in the parlor.

"I wanted to marry you. When we were kids."

"Then why didn't it happen?" I asked.

"Joe, he was the reason."

"You didn't have to take up with him."

"Maybe not. But Niccolò Jones, he told me he wanted some other kind of life."

"I was pie-eyed those days, I admit it, but you were wild. The second I left town."

"What was I supposed to do?"

"I heard stories."

"I was never going to be any college girl. I was never going to be long and slender. Not like that other one. Pearls and a silk skirt."

"You mean Anne?"

"Whatever her name. I didn't have her virtue. Or her money."

"You told me you would do anything to get me back."

"I did what I could. With what I had."

"Like marrying my brother?"

"You should've stopped me."

"I couldn't. Not once it started."

Marie reached over and lit the dinner candles on the table between us, and they reminded me of the candles a long time ago at the Church of Saints Peter and Paul.

"Let's eat this food," Marie said.

I was not comfortable in this domestic scene and neither was Marie. It was an echo of an old dream, something out of skew. Maybe because we wouldn't be sitting here like this if not for my brother's death. But then I had another drink and I ate a little bit more. The food was good and soon I was suffused with a combination of guilt and joy, exquisite stuff, and I forgot the earlier ugliness between us.

After dinner we took some air on the deck. It was a warm day for the city and we sat a long time above the ravine talking about things unimportant and inconsequential, like couples talk. At the end of the deck were the stairs that wound down into Telegraph Gardens, steep steps, with heavy metal edging. If Marie had slipped here, she was lucky not to have been hurt any worse. I glanced a moment more at the stairs and Marie glanced too, but neither of us said anything about them. Instead, we drank the wine and rocked in our chairs. Somewhere into the second bottle, I stood up and leaned against the back wall, then Marie came and leaned beside me, and we interlaced our fingers. Then I turned her around so her back was to me, and I slid my hands over hers, holding them at the wrists like manacles, and I kissed her on the neck. She arched around, her back still to me, and we kissed again one of those ferocious and forbidden kisses, the flat of my hand running down her soft blouse and into her skirt. Such embraces, dark and unwholesome, always excited us. Though Marie moaned and reached to touch me, she did not seem to want to take the moment any further, not now.

"Do you remember a conversation we had, before you went to law school? The night before?"

"Yeah."

"We talked about what we would do when you got back."

"I remember," I said.

"We would get a little house. It would be in a line of houses alongside all the other houses, and in the back there would be some fruit trees. Our child would play in the yard behind the sliding glass door. A little girl, running in the grass."

"I remember that little girl."

"And I would wear a blue dress, the color of the sky."

I caught the slightest touch of mockery in her voice. Directed at herself or me or both of us, I was not really sure.

"We were kids when we talked like that."

"But then you fell in love with Anne. She looked more like the woman in that picture."

"Marie, I didn't know what you were going to do next back then. And Joe . . . ."

"Don't talk about your brother. Why don't you take the job Micaeli wants to give you? It could make all the difference with us."

"Why?"

"You don't want a real living?"

She was right of course. Especially if we wanted to return to that moment when we could imagine those houses all in a line, the fruit trees and flowers so nice, everything bright as cellophane. Marie pulled away and went into the kitchen. I needed to piss. My dick was still hard and took a while to soften, but when the piss came out it was in a fierce golden arc. I zipped up. I turned the wrong way down the hall, my steps faltering outside her bedroom, and I could not help but glance in. The sheets were turned down, the room scented. I wondered if I would stay the night and I wondered too what would happen between us now that my brother was dead. I regarded the bed, the pillows, the open closet, the bookstand. On that bookstand, a photo album. I stepped in the room. Though it was none of my business, I picked up the album and flipped through.

The pictures went back to her early years with Joe. The kind of pictures you might expect. The two of them in the backyard patio, at home in Redwood City. On vacation, leaning against their car. Sitting on the stoop at my mother's place in North Beach. And there was my mother, her hair in a topknot, wearing one of those long dresses she'd taken to in her later years, still beautiful. And my father, leaning on his aluminum crutch, and myself too, hanging around, clowning at the fringe of things. Then landscapes, no people at all, Micaeli's house in Pescadore. The old man and his wife had opened their doors to her, not suspecting what was on everybody else's tongue. As time went forward, the color in the photographs changed, the images became more focused, sharper, and in that sharpness stood Joe again, looking lost and battered, during that time a few years back when they'd attempted to reconcile. Then two pages with missing photos, just black corners where the pictures had been.

Who had been on those missing photos? What images removed?

I turned the page. Marie alone. Places exotic and remote, Acapulco, maybe, or Hawaii.

Who was behind the camera, taking those pictures of Marie, traveling with her?

The possibilities irked me. I put the photo album away. And while I was doing that, bending down, I happened to see in her open wardrobe a pair of men's shoes. Italian loafers, pointed toes, dress leather, flouncey as hell, and expensive.

Michael Jr., I told myself. A hot dresser, the man behind the camera, they were the kind of shoes he would wear. Despite everything, nothing had changed. She was the same old Marie.

We ran into each other in the hall. She smiled but I did not give the smile back.

"The rumors, about you and Michael Jr., you know about those?"

I put my hand on her face and held her by the chin. A car passed on the street and its lights careened up the blinds.

"When was the last time you were with him?"

"I was never with him."

"Then whose shoes are those in your closet?"

"Shoes?"

"Men's shoes. I saw them in your closet."

"You're not so different than your brother. He always came up with wild ideas."

"Those shoes . . . ."

"Screw the shoes. You never been with anyone else, these past fifteen years? They never left anything in your apartment?"

"No," I lied.

She knew better. A small smirk turned on her lips, a matching one turned on mine, and that was the way it was between us. A draft of cold came through the sliding doors, all the way from Alcatraz.

"I'm sorry. It's just my brother's death, being here with you, all this. I'm not sure how to act. So I act some other way than who I am."

"Your brother was a louse. He wanted me because he knew that you were in love with me. And I was mad enough and bitter enough to let him do it. I paid like hell for that. I don't want to pay anymore."

"I'm sorry."

"You're not your brother. You don't have to act like him."

"My brother and I, we're like men in the mirror. He moves his right hand, I wiggle my left. He dies, and blood comes up my throat."

"Don't talk like that."

"I should go home. It's too soon for us."

But I didn't move. She leaned her head against my chest and I pushed my fingers through her hair.

"It doesn't have to be this way. We can live together. I'll wear that blue dress."

"Yeah."

"I meant what I said a long time ago. I'd do anything."

"How long do we have to be a secret?"

"I don't know. A year, six months. A decent time, so no one will talk. We owe ourselves that, a decent time."

"I don't care who talks."

"Only a little while. Till after Micaeli dies."

"What does he have to do with us?"

"He and Vincenza were good to me. And this, you and me, it would only confuse them. I don't want to hurt the old man."

Part of me balked, but I nodded my head. "All right." Though I still didn't understand what she was getting at, I told myself it didn't matter.

"There was never anything between his son and me."

"I believe you," I said.

The truth was I didn't know whether to believe her or not. At the moment it didn't much matter. Because we stood underneath the window now, another car was making the long climb, and I took Marie's face between my hands, kissing her violently in that falling light.

SEVENTEEN
THE HALL OF JUSTICE

If fate has compelled you in a gray and miserable direction, so that you are witness to things you should not know, or have done things you should not have done, then there is a room waiting down in the Hall of Justice. It is not a pleasant room. It is small and ugly, and in it sits an ugly table and some ugly chairs. The walls and floors seem deliberately misaligned, stained with the oil of human sweat, and the lighting flickers forever out of sync. It is an ugly room, poorly ventilated, in which people tell ugly truths. Since nothing goes on here but such talk, the accumulated ugliness can do nothing but accumulate further. Once you've been in such a room, you never leave it, because it is but an entryway to other such rooms, and even if by some mischance you walk free into the outer light you carry this room still inside your heart. Any unexpected thing, a glance from a stranger, a footfall on pavement, a jingle of keys, will bring you back, so that every other place seems an illusion, and you are faced again with this dirty ceiling, these dirty walls.

If we made our confessions in the open air, perhaps our guilt would float free and our crimes be forgotten. But in confines such as these, it is not only our own guilt we experience, but that of those who came before, and that of the world we carry within.

For me that was the world where old men got sloppy over their wine and spilled out the guts of the old days. My father mocked their stories, so I mocked them too, but I listened anyway to their talk of how it used to be. How when to be a Calibraze or Siciliane or Abruzzi was not the stuff of romance but the stuff of fish guts and poverty. It did not matter even if you were Genovesi and thought yourself superior, because you still stunk after you worked, and you could not change your clothes enough to escape that stink, or eat food which was not cheap and sloppy and mushed together, or change the fact that your native country *Oh terra bella! Oh patria mia!* was rife with stupidity.

Then came Mussolini. He of the magnificent voice and dismissive hand. Posters of Il Duce in the groceries and trattorias, all along Columbus Avenue, shrines and flowers.

But in the end, the devil got into Mussolini's ear. So the world fell into war.

The old ones loved to tell that story, lingering not on the war itself but on the last days of the illusion, before the fall was complete, when Mussolini drove through the Italian hills with Claratta Petacci at his side and their assassin had not yet been dispatched from Milan. As the storytellers moved toward the conclusion, and how the mob had ripped the lovers apart, their eyes would get weepy. They would catch you looking at them, little American, last name of Jones.

"Of course, he was a terrible man, Mussolini. A brute. The things those fascists did."

That did not stop them from finishing their story. Just as it did not stop the old men from swaggering the swagger of Mussolini, nor the old wives from crying the tears of betrayed women, nor the young women, wrapped in their American pearls, from turning their eyes towards the pictures of Claratta Petacci, imitating her brown-eyed pout and desiring her closet full of furs. No, all over North Beach, they were always telling it, the same story, the last days of Il Duce. It was the story in which everyone wanted a part. The old man, father of Italy. The young mistress. The jealous communist who murdered them both.

No, the communist said, I did it for justice. Because the fascists had betrayed Italy. Tortured our Italian brothers. Lined them up in firing squads. Violated our wives and daughters.

"Bah," said the old women. "You wanted Claratta for yourself."

I didn't know which was true, but I would think about it sometimes in my bed at night, just as I think about it now, inside this cell. I would imagine the young communist in his commandeered jeep, winding through the hills, taking Benito and Claratta from the cabin where they were hiding, marching them to the stone wall, holding up his gun, looking into those dark, fluttering eyes. I wondered then what I would do, if I would pull the trigger. And I knew, having come this far, the gun in my hand, there was no choice. The story needed its finish. The crowd was waiting in the square below.

In the end, those old Italians, all their stories ended the same.

EIGHTEEN
ANOTHER EVICTION

I itched to get out of town. I wanted to drive, to watch the scenery rise and fall outside the window. I called Marie and we made plans for the next day, to get out into the country.

Meanwhile I strolled around the old streets of the Beach. I did not see my surroundings so much as I saw imaginary other places, little paradises, where Marie and I might escape. I felt excitement at the idea of leaving, if only for the day, perhaps the same excitement the other sons and daughters of my parents' generation had felt when they made preparations to clear out for good. It was only the oldest ones left now and the hangers-on. Leaving was something I should have done a long time ago. I hadn't the nerve then, but a second chance was coming. Things were circling around again for Marie and me. All I had to do was take what Micaeli was offering. Talk to his son. Be patient. Before long I would be respectable again. Other opportunities would follow. A man keeps his eyes open, that's what happens. We'd leave the Beach at last and find a little place to the south, or north, it didn't matter, someplace with a palm and a golden hill, where old Italians didn't exist.

But nothing changes overnight and I still had some work to do for Jimmy Wong. A building of his, a three-story walk-up near Jackson Square, was scheduled for demolition. Only an old Chinese man on the first floor wouldn't leave. Usually Jimmy saved the Chinese evictions for his own people, but he was in a crunch and didn't want the Chinese neighbors to see him throwing out one of his own.

Anyway, the old man was no plum. I'd been through it with him a couple of times before. He'd shouted at me in Chinese, refused to open the door, and wouldn't let me serve him with the papers.

So I brought Rickie and Eddie Lee and told them we might have to bust open the door on this one, just drag the old man's stuff into the street. Inside we ran into an unexpected difficulty. The old man had his grandson with him, a burly kid maybe twenty-five years old, thick through the shoulders, long black hair and a Fu Manchu mustache. He wore a kimono over his jeans and t-shirt.

"You're a son of a bitch," the kid told me.

"It's not my idea. You know Jimmy Wong? It's his property." I dug into my pocket and pulled out a couple of dimes. "There's a phone booth on the corner. If Jimmy tells you okay, then okay."

My plan was to get the Lee brothers started while the grandson was out looking for a phone. I gave the kid my sincerest look but apparently it wasn't sincere enough.

"Just talk to Jimmy. He's a reasonable man."

"I'm not moving."

"He's your people."

"You don't understand, do you? It's not a race issue, it's class."

The streets here had been filled with kids like him, maybe ten, fifteen years back. ABC's, the old Chinese called them. American Born Chinese. College-educated, amateur communists out for a weekend with the ancestors. I remembered them carrying the red flag down Kearny Street while the old Chinamen—who hated Mao more than they hated the dirt itself—yelled curses from the thin-railed balconies above, heaping over chicken guts and old vegetables, all the refuse of Chinatown.

The kid in the kimono tried to argue with me. Meanwhile his grandfather, wearing a plaid shirt and green khakis, paced back and forth among the half-packed boxes. From the looks of the apartment, and the expression on the old man's face, it seemed the grandfather knew the situation was hopeless and didn't want to fight us anymore. The grandson though had worked himself into a brand-new frenzy.

"You fucking assholes, throwing my grandfather out just for an extra buck."

"Come on, kid. The building's empty. No one lives here anymore. It's going to be torn down."

"This should be housing for the old. We don't need another office building."

"I don't know anything about that."

The truth was I didn't much care what Jimmy did with his buildings. The building, sandwiched between Chinatown and North Beach, was in the shadow of the TransAmerica Pyramid. Whether Wong wanted to put offices here, or high-rise apartments, it wasn't my concern.

"I checked the permit applications, it belongs to High Wind enterprises."

"So?"

"It is a joint venture, Ellipse and Far West."

And as the kid began to talk, going on with the interconnections—TransAmerica owned by Merrill Lynch transferred to Far West Holding through Singapore Incorporated via Chevron and Bechtel through the Suez Canal courtesy of Marco Polo—I heard somewhere in there the name of Micaeli Romano's holding firm, and I realized that this deal involved Romano as well as Jimmy Wong, and I smiled to myself because it had never occurred to me they might work together (and were probably working together on China Basin too), but of course it would be true, because this was the way of business, and after all it was a small world and even smaller neighborhood.

Rickie and Eddie Lee were getting anxious and a little bored. They came up behind me and tried to engage the kid in some dialogue.

"Shut up, punk."

"Shut up yourself," the kid said, brave as hell. But his hands were shaking, and Rickie and Eddie began edging him into the far room.

I used the distraction to squeeze past the boy to the grandfather. The old man had moved away from the main action and was looking down at things that were the things of his life. To be honest, there wasn't a whole lot there. A black and white TV. Some bags full of this and that, a glass Buddha, a portrait of his wife. His grandkid was still bellowing somewhere behind us and the situation was getting heated. I motioned to the old man, suggesting we step out on the porch. Outside I handed him a room key with a little ticket attached, and on it written in Chinese was the name of the Ling Wei Hotel. I pointed at the truck and told him we would be down with his stuff later, and that Jimmy Wong had come up with a week's rent for him, and it was nice at the Ling Wei, every bit as nice as this place, with running water and a clever little stove for heating tea. Then I gave him thirty-five bucks, again courtesy of Jimmy Wong, and pointed to the hotel ticket and told him to go. He hesitated, glancing inside to where his grandson was still arguing with the other two Chinese. There was a look of concern on the old man's face, but I gave him the gentle hand on the shoulder and off he went. I lit up a cigarette and watched him walk away, out into the crosswalk, his eyes fixed on the Ling Wei up ahead.

The grandkid was right, of course. It was money behind it all. Nothing to do with who you were or where you came from. It was money made the whole difference, and bought you your dreams, and there was no sense in letting skin color or any kind of romance tell you different. It was the fact of things, like it or not, and if you couldn't accept it, then you would get what the grandkid was about to get from Rickie and Eddie, who had their own frustrations with this life and got their pleasure where they could.

Late that afternoon I went up to the Pyramid for my appointment with Michael Jr. His office overlooked the neighborhood, the pastel apartments and concrete gardens of North Beach. He smiled and shook my hand, clasping it between both of his at once, a gesture startlingly similar to that of his father in its force and warmth. His features too were animated with the same spirit as Micaeli's, so that any physical difference between himself and his adoptive father did not seem so great as it might have been, as if his appearance itself had been reshaped by lifelong proximity to the older man.

He gestured for me to sit down but instead I took a long look at his feet.

"What?"

"Your shoes."

"Yes?"

"I been looking to get myself a new pair."

"Ox-blood. I just bought them."

"Very nice."

"Thank you."

"You ever wear the Italian ones, you know. With the sharp toes. And the little bibs?"

"What? Oh, those. Not too durable. And not exactly our generation."

"Sharp though."

"Yes. A bit too sharp. They make a man look as if he has cloven feet."

We both got a little laugh out of that. Then Michael Jr. got down to business, telling me more or less what his father had told me the week before in Pescadore. Various parties were coming together to swing the China Basin deal, along with the main backers from Hong Kong, and my job would be to work with a team of lawyers trying to keep the deal from blowing up because the people in neighborhoods didn't like the design, or the city didn't like the contractors, or any one of a thousand other reasons. He went on with the details, and I remembered for the first time in a long time why I had lost interest in the pursuit of the law. I gave him the wide-eyed look, nodding my head like a junior partner, but the truth was I was still thinking about his shoes and wondering if he had lied.

"Several of the principals will be in Sausalito in a couple of days, at my father's place. I'm going to be out of town, but he wants you there. Shake hands with the Hong Kong money."

"What time?"

"About eleven, on Tuesday. It'll be brunch. You don't have to say much, just take it in." He checked me over for a second, up and down. "Go to Stephano's, have yourself outfitted. We have an account there. You should wear a suit."

"I'll even take a bath."

"Same old Nick." He laughed, strained as hell, patting me on the back. "A million laughs."

For an instant the mask cracked and I could see beneath his charm, which after all was not really his charm but his father's, and it wasn't hard to tell he had reservations about the whole damned thing and thought the old man was crazy for letting a man like me inside the family door.

NINETEEN
EXIT PARADISE

The next morning I dandied on one of the new shirts I'd picked up from Stephano's, crisp and white, and a new pair of slacks. I met Marie on a corner at the edge of the neighborhood and drove south. We kept the windows open. I had not drunk anything the night before, and the morning air was invigorating. I caught Marie regarding me, enjoying my unrumpled and healthy look, and as we moved out of the fog down the peninsula I felt the weight of Little Italy fall away.

We headed down 101, driving through all the little towns that had become one big town. Milbrae and San Bruno and Daly City. Sunnyvale and Mountain View. Sweeping past the ragged little stuccos that sat hunched alongside the freeway. Past the bowling alleys and motels on one side, the mudflats on the other, where dozers shoveled concrete fill for new industrial parks. We kept going further south, away from the bay, off the peninsula and into the valley, past more of the same stucco houses, the same hotels and industrial parks, then past them all one more time, then yet once again, before the landscape broke open and the road narrowed as in some not-so-distant past and there were orchards to either side. The city was gone behind us, we had left the freeway, but the traffic was still fast. The cars ahead set the pace, the ones behind made sure you did not falter, and the oncoming traffic came at us through some skewed geometry.

"Where did you go when you left town?" Marie asked. "You never told me."

"Reno," I said.

I caught a glimpse of another driver, like myself, straining for a look at the countryside, wanting to enter it but unable to do so, driven forward by some inner energy over which he had little control. Marie flinched. "What were you doing in Reno?"

"Client work," I lied. "Divorce." I didn't want her to know what I'd been doing. There was no sense to it, and it had all led nowhere anyway.

"I didn't know you were doing that kind of work."

"Sometimes," I said.

She turned her head away from me, and looked out at the landscape. We were still hurtling forward, propelled by the traffic.

"I'd like to take a walk," she said.

"Me too."

"Then let's get out of this damned car."

"I'm doing my best."

There were no turn outs and I had to thrust the car forward onto the shoulder, fishtailing through the gravel and the high yellow dust. I killed the engine when we hit the scrub on the side of the road.

We were somewhere south of San Jose, in an old valley tucked between the hills, overgrown with oak and grass. Beyond the scrub was a creek with a path running alongside. The creek was dry and to one side stood an apricot orchard and on the other lay wild land.

We followed the path up the dry bed, Marie first, myself just a few steps behind. She wore a white blouse and red slacks and big silver earrings. Now that I'd come to see my brother's death as an act of fate, not part of conspiracy, I didn't see much reason to hold back anymore. He'd been a son of a bitch to her anyway, I told myself, and a burden round my neck. The sun was hot overhead, the insects chuttered in the grass, and I felt my desire more fiercely the further we walked. Some Mexican families worked under the apricot trees ahead, splitting the harvested fruit with long knives. A young boy smeared the apricots with sulfur, then lay them to dry in a wooden tray. I could hear the flies swarm from a hundred yards down the path.

The Mexicans watched as we walked by, pretending to still be at their labor, but I could see in the men's eyes they were regarding Marie, and I could see, too, the women regarding me, and I imagined that the heat and desire between Marie and me was such that other people could not help but notice and desire us too. I cursed myself for all the time I had allowed to pass bound up and tied by filial loyalty.

"Let's keep going," I said. "Away from the people."

Her blouse was damp, and there was sweat on her brow. There was sweat too on my clean shirt, and I felt good walking under the sun, and strong and young.

The path curved away from the dry bank, through the far edge of the orchard, alongside a copse of willows. Our view to the east was obscured by them, and I saw an old water tower rising in their midst. I wanted to stop and rest under those willows, to lay in the soft grass beside Marie and touch her blouse and taste her lips that would split open like an apricot, and her tongue that was like the soft fruit inside. But Marie kept walking, more furiously. I sensed something bothering her.

I kept following, catching through the willows an occasional glimpse of the orchard beyond. It had to be an underground spring feeding the willows, I thought, the trees were so lush and green.

At last we made it around the copse. Marie was maybe fifty yards ahead of me. She paused at the peak of a nearby rise, then disappeared. I hurried forward, then saw Marie below me on a path snaking through the orchard. At the end of the path were houses. They looked to be new houses, built in the last year or so, and the streets were fresh and black. In the orchard you could see the surveyor's lines: the small sticks and red flags and white string marking out how the street would continue on and join the highway back where we had parked. I caught up to Marie and we looked at the houses, how the street just stopped in the middle of that orchard. Some kids played on the street in front of the houses, a hawk circled overhead, and I wanted Marie more than ever: to take her inside one of those houses and lay with her on the floor and listen to the cry of that hawk and the sound of those children playing. I put my arm around her, gently, and she picked that moment to break down, crying like a maniac.

"Everything will be all right," I said.

"No, it won't."

"Why not?"

"Why did you go to Reno?" she asked again.

"I told you."

She looked up at me, and I looked at her, and it came to me that she knew I had been lying.

"Why do you ask?"

"Just don't leave me alone like that. Please."

She buried her head into my chest, and I stood there with my arms around her. The kids took a look in our direction and scampered inside. Overhead, the hawk plunged into the orchard then flew up again, clutching something dead in its beak.

TWENTY
MORE LEANORA CHINN

The next afternoon I lay in the grass in Washington Square contemplating my future and the shape it might take. I could come to no conclusions. Someone from the North Beach Chamber of Commerce had raised an Italian flag from the roof of a nearby building, here in the heart of the old neighborhood, but the truth was you'd be hard pressed to find any of the old faces. The park was full, but not with Italians. Some Chinese kids, dressed in the uniform of the Salesian school, rolled and tumbled beneath the magnolias. A Mexican woman and her daughter mugged for an old man's camera. A Viet teenager, legs smooth and long, stopped in front of me and bent down, snuffing a cigarette against her heel. A pretty black boy in drag straddled a nearby bench, puckering his lips and complimenting the men who walked by. Soon he was gone and the others were gone too, in and out of the park, and new people came to take their place. The wind ruffled across the grass, and I could see the grass trembling with the inconstancy of it all, and even the buildings seemed to offer but the illusion of permanence. They had shifted and fallen before, then been raised again after earthquakes and fire, so that the park itself was not in the same place it had once been, and over it all was the Italian flag, with no Italians in sight. I dozed in the balmy air, face down on the grass, and in my dreams the shadows and shapes of the world shifted past one another, and I was filled with an intolerable longing, and a sense of approaching calamity. When I woke, the breeze had stopped. The Italian flag hung still on its pole, unrecognizable, and I felt oddly at peace with the world.

The feeling didn't last.

When I got home, Leanora Chinn stood on the stoop out front of the building. She wore the same blue skirt, the same blue blouse, and she held a manila envelope in her hand.

"You're looking clear-eyed," she said.

She took my hand with a firm shake and glimmered me up and down, partly in the way of a cop, but also in a way a woman looks at you when she has her doubts and wonders how it is a guy like you gets by in the world. I guessed she knew about my line of employment by now. And about my brushes with vice.

"Thanks," I said.

"New clothes?"

"Yeah."

I wanted to tell her she was wrong about me. Things were going well, my life was changing around. But I knew cops were suspicious of good news, so I kept my cheery disposition to myself.

"I have something I need to discuss with you."

"About Joe?"

"Yes."

"He was drugging it?" I asked.

Chinn cast her eyes away from me. She wore no makeup and I could see the thin veins on her lids and a small puckering mark where she bit into her upper lip. She was silent and I was stupid, reading her silence the wrong way.

"I guessed it from the first," I said, "though I didn't want to admit it. Not right away. You know how it is, after something like this happens, you don't want to believe it was somehow their fault. The loved one's. You want to think . . . ."

"No. That's not it."

"No?"

"We have some new information."

I felt a small hammer of disappointment beating in my wrists, and in my head. Over the past few days my attitude had changed, and I preferred the cops just slam the door on my brother's death.

"We have an undercover man working this case."

"You mentioned that."

"He's checked all his contacts in the Mission and listened to all the talk. Your brother wasn't making change with the dealers down there. A little pot, maybe, but nothing else."

"So it was just bad luck. A robbery."

"We don't think that either."

"Oh."

Maybe she heard the disappointment in my voice, or maybe I was just guilty over the grief I didn't feel. Either way Lieutenant Chinn looked me up and down again, and I got the sense she knew everything Marie and I had done the last few days, all the details of my past. Standing there on the street in my new pressed slacks and white shirt, I felt there wasn't anything I could do to hide the small ugliness in my heart. I wanted to say I hadn't done anything, I was innocent. It was true enough I guess. Unless you counted coveting your brother's wife. Or taking a job with the man who'd screwed your mother backwards and forwards before the war.

"How can I help you, Lieutenant Chinn? I'll do anything to help."

"I have some things I want to show you."

"Sure. Let's go up to my room."

"Not there."

"To the station?"

My voice trembled. Maybe I was already thinking ahead to that grimy little room under the Hall of Justice.

"We don't have to go the station, not unless you want to. I was thinking of a place a little more relaxed. Up here. The other side of Grant."

"All right."

"Have you had lunch?"

"I can always have more."

I walked with her across Columbus Avenue, past the Ling Wei Hotel and into Chinatown. We jostled down Stockton Street, where the crowds are always shoulder-to-shoulder, and the shop bins are filled with plastic chopsticks and paper fans and nylon kimonos, and the grocery windows are strung with half-cooked chickens, plucked and shiny, hanging from their bright red feet. Up above, in the second story knock-outs, the women were working behind sewing machines, just as they have worked forever, only these days they were competing with sweatshops in Bangkok and Hong Kong, and the little spools of thread spun on their spindles deep into the night.

I followed her into a small coffee shop where the booths

were red upholstery, and an old Chinese woman served dirt-brown coffee in white cups that had a thin film of oil on top and tasted as old-fashioned bad as coffee anywhere in America. Leanora Chinn and the waitress spoke loudly and familiarly, some kind of a Cantonese dialect. The old woman managed to pour my coffee without her eyes so much as traveling across my face.

"We found a man with a connection to your brother."

"What kind of connection?"

"We're not sure yet. Could be coincidence."

"Who is this man?"

"He's got half a dozen names. Or had half a dozen names. He's dead now."

"Dead?"

"They recovered his body about a week back. In an ice box, behind a fish house down on Grant Street. It took us a while to come up with an ID."

I felt a small thrill at the notion of this dead man packed in ice, behind a restaurant in Chinatown, and the idea my brother had been involved with him somehow. It seemed to suggest how far wrong my brother had turned, and in that way relieved me of the guilt I felt about moving in on Marie. He'd been up to something stupid, my brother, some dumb-fuck routine.

"Lee Chow, Mark Nai, Naikon Lee, Minh Ho. Those were some of the dead man's aliases. Sound familiar?"

"No."

"He was a young man, maybe thirty. Part Vietnamese, part Chinese, scorned by either culture. He did dirty jobs around town. For money, of course."

"What kind of dirty jobs?"

"He killed people. He was an assassin. Old Chinese profession," she said. "Italian, too."

The waitress came with more coffee. The two of them spoke a while in Chinese, exuberantly, as if I were not there. Leanora pointed at my cup for the woman to pour, and the old waitress did so once again without looking at me or acknowledging my existence, as if she were watering a plant.

"I ordered you some chop suey. It's their specialty. The best in Chinatown."

"Great," I said. "My favorite."

The truth was I hated chop suey, I could not even stand to look at it on my plate. When the waitress was gone, Leanora undid the clasp on the manila envelope. She took out a set of glossies, put them carefully on top of the envelope, then slid the whole thing towards me.

"You know him?"

The top picture looked to have been taken after the corpse had been discovered, when the man still lay in the ice box. The face was discolored but his eyes were open and the features discernible. His looks were familiar, but I wasn't quite sure and decided to keep the similarities to myself.

"He was strangled with piano wire before they dumped him in the box."

"Never seen him."

I started to slide the pictures back but Chinn shook her head.

"Keep looking."

I flipped to the next glossy. It was a full head shot of the guy, taken down at the morgue I guessed, and I shrugged at Chinn, and she nodded, and I flipped again. Next was a series of mug shots taken when the guy was still alive. Front profile. Rear. Side. If I had any doubts before, I didn't now. I recognized him all right. He was the man behind the door where Jimmy Wong had sent me to deliver the black leather valise, down the alleyway, the day before my brother's death.

"You recognize him?"

I shook my head.

"Sorry."

"Look at the last one."

On the final page, lined up on a single sheet, were several Polaroids of my brother. They were a few years old and showed him on a deck somewhere, palms and eucalyptus rising in the background. He was smiling, very aggressively, but there was a look of confusion and sadness in his face too. It was a look I'd seen a lot these last few years as he struggled to get control over things that continually slipped away.

"Do you know where those were taken?"

"No. I've never seen those pictures before."

"Looks like he's somewhere in the city."

"Those eucalyptus could be anywhere in California," I said.

"Not that house on the other side of the grove. The yellow Victorian."

"That's a common style."

"Not that cornice," she insisted. "It's very unusual."

She let the pictures sit there in front of me, the picture of the murdered Indo-Chinese and the Polaroids of my brother. I tried to avoid looking either at Chinn or the pictures. My eyes skittered around the cafe. The old woman moved slowly behind the counter, pouring coffee one customer at a time. The place was quiet except for the mumbling of an old Chinese man who sat alone in one of the booths.

"What are you doing with these pictures of my brother?"

"We found them in the dead man's apartment."

"The one in the ice box?"

"He had a number of pictures in a drawer in his kitchen. Pictures of different people. We checked around, all these people, they're dead. Murdered."

"You think he killed my brother?"

"We think somebody paid him to do it."

The little hammer was beating in my wrists again, harder than before. I could feel it in my chest, too, and in my head. I thought of myself walking down that alley with the black valise in my hand, and I saw again that valise sitting in Micaeli Romano's office, and the empty picture page in Marie's portfolio, and the angle of the landscape behind my brother's head in the picture that lay in front me. Marie's deck, I thought, that's where he's sitting, in the same spot I had been the other night. It was clear to me now, though I did not want it to be clear. I felt the blood rushing from my face, and the hammering, and that pale dizziness that overcomes you when the world seems no longer real. In the background was the strange muttering of the old Chinese man, the shuffling of the old waitress moving infinitely slowly, carrying two plates now, coming toward us. Leanora Chinn, dressed in her crisp blue blouse, leaned forward, regarding me from behind the porcelain mask of her face. There was something in the depths of those almond eyes, a small little window of light.

"Are you all right?" Her voice was soft, full of concern. I was tempted to reveal to her whatever I knew, but I gave it a second thought and held my tongue.

"I'm just trying to take this in."

"Of course."

"Is there any connection between the different people this man killed?"

"Not that we can see. They all just had somebody that wanted them dead. A relative maybe, a wife, a business associate."

"I see."

"Do you know why anyone would want to kill your brother?"

"No. Have you spoken with Luisa? His widow. She saw him every day. A lot more than me."

"She took her kids to Sacramento. To live with relatives. But we don't regard her as a suspect. And she doesn't seem to know anything about his life away from the house."

I could hear the waitress behind me, very close now. Chinn gathered up the photos, making way for the plates.

"We came across some domestic violence reports from a few years back. The first wife and your brother. Police in Redwood City were over to their place a couple times. But nothing with Luisa."

"They are different women. He was older," I said. "And that earlier, it was divorce stuff. Posturing for the courts."

I don't know why I stuck up for him that way, just because he was my brother. Maybe I thought it was true, or what had happened back then had been my fault underneath it all. The waitress put down our food, two plates of chop suey.

126

"You don't have any idea where the pictures of your brother might have been taken? Or who took them?"

I hesitated.

"No," I said.

I started in on my plate. It tasted like any chop suey I had ever had. I couldn't stomach it but I ate it anyway, ferociously, as if it were the last food in the world.

"You like it?"

"It's delicious."

"I've been eating here since I was a kid."

"It's the best I ever had," I said. "Makes me want to visit China."

"I've been. The food isn't as good there."

"I bet."

With the arrival of the food, Chinn loosened up. Either that or she was pretending to loosen so as to catch me off guard. She dropped the matter of the pictures and talked instead about the Chinese situation in the city. How the old bachelor society was almost gone now, that class of Chinese men who had labored and grown old in San Francisco, never marrying because Chinese women had not been allowed to immigrate. She talked about those sad old men and about the new immigrants, the poor ones from the mainland and the rich ones from Hong Kong. How the tongs, the old criminal syndicates, were enjoying a revival now, with the trade in heroin and smuggling of illegal immigrants. How the Indo-Chinese tongs were the most violent, made up of Southeast Asians, mixed race, scorned by everyone, and how they brought with them from Cambodia and Vietnam their old rivalries, and their old ways of fighting those rivalries. All these different groups, they had their politics and their figureheads, she said. They had their Maos and their Chiang Kais, their Ho Chis and Madame Ngus. Yes, I thought, they all have their Il Duces, whom they argue over night and day, weeping and hollering, and whose pictures hang on the bedroom walls. Then Chinn told me that the young Indo-Chinese who'd killed my brother had been an informer for the Pathet Lao during the Vietnam War. He'd been killed, she suspected, by a Vietnamese street gang.

"How do you know?"

"They left their mark carved on his body."

"He was a member of a rival gang?"

"No. He operated independently."

"They didn't approve of his business?"

"Maybe. Or maybe they just didn't like his color."

We left the restaurant and as we walked she pointed out little bits of Chinatown history, old opium corners, crib houses, she was full of this kind of thing, then suddenly we were halfway up Kai-Chin alley and she was gesturing down at the old stones.

"This alley here, there is a picture of it, from early in the century. Chinese men in black capes. They called it the Street of Gamblers."

We stood in front of the door where I had dropped off the valise Jimmy Wong had given me, and I looked at the door, and Leanora Chinn looked at me, and I saw it was no accident that she had guided me down this alley. She was studying my reaction to see if I knew this place. I kept my face as empty as I could.

"Something else," Chinn asked. "Did your brother know anyone in Reno?"

"Not that I know of." I avoided looking her in the eye. She was coming at me from too many angles. "Why do you ask?"

"We found some ticket stubs in his room. Credit card reports. It seems he went there not long before he died."

"I don't know anything about that," I said. "I have to get hurrying. There's things I have to do."

As we walked out of the alley, Leanora Chinn was quiet. I felt burly alongside her. She was a small woman really, delicate, in her midnight skirt and her dark blouse, and as we emerged out of the alley into the pagodas and glitter of Grant Street, I was tempted again to divulge to her all the things I knew, to make a breast of it before it was too late. Instead I shook her hand at the corner and disappeared as fast as I could into the crowd along Columbus Avenue.

128

TWENTY-ONE
THE ENEMY WITHIN

It was sunset and an orange light filled the sky. I sat in the graying shadows of that light, at my desk, and studied my wall of ancestors. My mother's Aunt Angela in her peasant dress. Her uncle Tony, arms crossed in front of his belly, legs big as tree stumps. My grandparents and great grandparents standing in a wheatfield in the middle of the Abruzzi nowhere, back home in Italy. I had pictures of these people but no memories because they'd never come to America. They were the ancestors I had never known, and their images hung on the wall alongside pictures of yellow fields I had never seen, and postcards from Italian cities whose names I could not pronounce.

Among them hung photos of myself and my brother and my parents too, standing in front of our Chevys and Fords, hands on the door handles, as if ready to launch ourselves into that sun whose reflected light was fading this minute from the windows of the TransAmerica Pyramid. Only in those pictures, we did not yet seem convinced we were ready for any such journey.

They had no advice for us then, those ancestors, and no advice for me now.

The way Chinn had taken me down that alley, reading my face the whole time, it was no coincidence. The longer I thought about it, the more I figured the cops had gone up and down Kai-chin alley not just with my brother's photo but with mine too, looking to see if anybody recognized me. Maybe someone had. Maybe someone had seen me walk up to that yellow door and hand the valise inside. If so, it would look to the cops like I had arranged the murder.

Maybe that's the way it was supposed to look. I told myself the Romanos were behind this. From what Chinn had told me, I knew my brother had gone to Reno. Joe had been onto something after all, I guessed, and he had tried to use it, to make sure he got a piece of the China Basin deal. Only the Romanos wouldn't be blackmailed. Michael Jr. had lifted the photos of Joe from the album in Marie's apartment during one of his visits, I guessed. Then he and the old man had sent the money and photos to Jimmy Wong, who'd passed them along to me. They'd managed it so I'd delivered the hit message on my own brother, handing the whole package to the assasin, and now there was nothing I could do.

If I went to the police with this story, how would I prove it? Romano had his valise back and all the evidence pointed to me.

So I couldn't go to Chinn. And I didn't feel like I could tell Marie either, because she wanted me to take Romano's job, and I didn't want to bring everything crashing down around us. The easiest way would be to play dumb. Just take Micaeli's offer. Act like I thought it came from the goodness of his heart. It was tempting, I had to admit. Because Marie would be mine and the old man was dying anyhow, and I could get my revenge against him the easy way, by going back later and spitting on his grave.

Even so, I didn't know if I could keep the truth balled up inside me like that, knowing that Romano had been the one behind it. How he'd arranged my brother's death and made it so the blood was on my hands too, carrying that money down the alley.

I didn't know what to do. So I studied my wall of ancestors for a while, then I searched out the old article I'd lifted from Johnny Bruno's place, the one about Pavrotti's death. I found nothing in it I hadn't already gone over in my head, so I went back to the clipping from the real estate section and tried to decipher the figures my brother had scrawled on the other side over the obituaries. The writing was in pencil, barely legible, and I copied the figures over onto a fresh piece of paper, one letter at a time, one number, but they still did not mean much to me.

AR—Ren 130; Lv Mon 2

Then I lay down on the bed with the clipping in my hands. Out of idleness really, for no other reason, I began to read the obituaries, and as I did so, I had reason to sit up suddenly. I noticed something I had not noticed before. A faint circle, drawn in pencil, around the name of one of the dead men.

Billy Dios, Reno.

The obit was nothing much, a simple paragraph announcing the death of a man named Billy Dios, formerly of North Beach, age 78, who'd died in Nevada of natural causes. Survived by two daughters, it said, though it gave neither of their names.

Dios, though, that part of it clicked in my head. I felt for a moment that feeling you get when things suddenly juxtapose—weightless, dizzy, an enthusiasm in the chest— a sudden knowledge of the inevitable, that makes you feel powerful, Mr. Somebody, rubbing elbows with fate, until you realize you are only a watcher, hopeless in the face of what will happen next. In the middle of this headiness, all frothed up, I went back to the article I had lifted from Johnny Bruno. There it was again. Forty years ago, a North Beach man by the name of Dios had been held for questioning in connection with the death of Pavrotti. It came to me then just as it must have come to my brother.

Dios and Ciprione were the same man.

I looked at the scrawled notes on the real estate clipping, and at last I realized what they were. Flight numbers. Arrival time and departure. Joe had called the flight operator with the obituary in his hand and made notes on the back side. He'd hunted up Johnny Bruno, keeping his suspicions to himself, feeling him out for information about the past. Then he'd flown to Reno to see what he could find.

Joe had found Ellen Ciprione, I was almost sure. And he'd gotten something to use against Romano. Nothing else made any sense.

I wanted to be sure, though, because the medical records in Reno had identified the dead man as Ciprione, not Dios. So I dialed up Reno information, then I called the daughter. She picked up on the third ring, her voice sultry with alcohol.

"Hello."

"Yes," I said, putting on my lawyer's voice from the old days. I could still find it, sometimes, when I needed to. "I'm looking for an Ellen Dios."

There was a hesitation on the other side. "What is this in regards too?" she asked.

"An inheritance. The estate of Billy Dios. He had an insurance policy, naming his daughter as beneficiary."

It was nonsense, of course. There was no policy, but I wanted to get her to admit her father's other name. She did it more quickly than I expected, drawn out by the smell of money. If she'd been sober—or if she could have seen my face—probably she would have shut me down sooner than she did.

"My father was Billy Dios. But he changed his name to Ciprione. Before I was born."

"I see," I said.

I didn't say anything for a while. There was a small silence while I contemplated my next move. That was my mistake. Not thinking it out in advance before I called, but instead rushing headlong with the moment, and now wondering what to say. In that silence I could feel her growing suspicious.

"Who is this?" she asked.

"An insurance adjuster. I . . . ."

"Bullshit," she said. Then she hung up.

I had lost her. Maybe I could have played Ellen Ciprione differently, I thought, but probably it didn't matter. She was a clever one, or if not clever, naturally suspicious, and your only chance with someone like her was to get her drunk up close and personal, and then hope she wasn't a mean drunk. Anyway, it was too late for that. At least I knew for certain Ciprione and Dios were the same man, and I could be pretty certain my brother knew it too. Joe had been to Reno, tracking down Romano's past, and he'd found something the old man didn't want him to know. About the old fascist business, maybe. About Romano's connection to Billy Dios. So the Romano clan had had him killed. I was sure of that now, or almost sure. Even so, my elation from a few minutes before, that was gone. Because knowing what was up, and proving it, these were two different things. The more I thought about it, the more I realized old man Romano was still safe. He'd fixed it so there wasn't anything I could reveal without implicating myself. After all, I was the one who had delivered the money, and that was the only thing the cops would see.

*   *   *

Later that evening the phone rang. It was Marie, her voice taut and silky, filled with pleasure, anticipating our new life.

"We still on for tomorrow?"

"Of course," I said, because I didn't know what else to say, and I still wanted her.

"I'll bring dinner. I'll come up the back stairs to your apartment, so no one will see. That's a good idea, don't you think?"

"Double good," I said.

"We'll have a nice time, a nice dinner. Then I'll leave early and let you rest."

"You don't have to do that."

"It's a big day for you Tuesday. You're going to Micaeli's, remember? To meet with the men from Hong Kong. Your first day on the job."

"I'm excited," I said.

"You should be."

"But I want you to stay with me tomorrow night. Give me a send-off."

"Like a rocket ship."

We cooed back and forth like that on the phone for a while, whispering sweet sounds into one another's ears, and though I didn't really believe any of it, hers or mine, that sweetness lingered even after we got off. I told myself what the hell difference did it make. I could dress up in a white shirt and a tie and take the drive over to Sausalito and play the old man's game, hell, take his money, pretend nothing had happened. What did it really matter how my brother had died after all? It was only my life that mattered now. I took a drink, then another one, and blew smoke out the open window and wondered how long I would be able to keep myself happy with that idea.

133

TWENTY-TWO
LAST HAPPINESS

Marie stood in my living room holding a bag of groceries. She had made herself over and was self-conscious as hell. She wore a blue dress, a string of pearls around the collar, her hair dyed chestnut brown like it used to be, so it curled up in a schoolgirl kind of flip. She smiled and I remembered a different kind of passion, one I had felt when I was younger and more innocent and did not fear so much that the pleasures of the world would pass me by. Marie's smile faded as she stood there, as if she could read in my face that darkness passing over me.

"Has something happened?"

"No," I said.

"Should I not be here?"

"You look beautiful."

"You don't mean that."

"I do. You're the most beautiful woman in the world."

It was silly stuff but Marie liked it. She ditched the groceries and put a finger beneath my belt, tugging me towards her. I wore my new slacks from Stephano's and we kissed each other in our wholesome clothes. Then she went into the kitchen. She yanked an apron out of her bag and I helped her put it on, running my hands up over her breasts and my fingers under the collar of the blue dress and pushing lewdly against her while she reached down where polite girls are not supposed to reach. Then she went back to her vegetables.

That's the way the evening went. All over each other one moment, then demure as hell. We set the table and touched each other and put spoons in one another's mouths and our hands beneath one another's clothing. We talked about where we would go and the things we would do and how we would live our lives. Except every once in a while I would think of the fraud that lay underneath it all, that son of a bitch Romano, and a cloud would darken my face and she would see that cloud.

"What's wrong?" she asked.

"Nothing."

"Then how come the five days of gloom on your face?"

I went again to the window and gandered down at the street. On Columbus Avenue old man Zirpoli was standing in front of his news store like he'd done every day of his life, like his father had done before him. Meanwhile the street hustlers were weaving among the tourists, pickpockets and camera thieves looking for a bit of work, and an old woman held a dead chicken by the neck as she wound her way into Chinatown.

Marie leaned out beside me.

"Same old streets," she said. "Nothing changes."

"It's changed."

"I don't know. Old man Zirpoli's still out in front of his shop. It still says Molini on the deli window. There's still the drunk beatniks on the corner. It looks like the same old streets to me."

She was right but then she was wrong. Zirpoli could stand in front of his newsstand until Mussolini rose from the dead, but the truth was Molini's deli was up for sale, his kids had moved to East Jesus, and there was no such place as North Beach anymore.

"Don't be so blue," she said. "You take that job, six months, we can move a little bit away. Maybe the other side of the bridge."

"I'm not blue."

I smiled, pert as hell, and took another drink. We toasted one another there in the window and just then Zirpoli happened to glance up. He yelled at us in Italian and Marie yelled back.

"Ah, like old times, to see people young and beautiful leaning from their window," he said.

"Yes, and just like old times, we are getting ready to leave this place forever."

Some tourists the other side of Columbus watched our little scene, charmed.

"Let's raise our glasses to them," Marie said.

"All right."

We raised our wine glasses. They got out their cameras.

"Let's laugh."

So I laughed and she laughed and the cameras clicked away. I could hear the shutters flashing across six lanes of traffic.

"We look the Italian couple."

"Let's kiss," she said.

We did it first for the tourists, a joke, then passionately, tongues deep in one another's mouths, so that when we looked back the gawkers, embarrassed, had turned their heads. Old man Zirpoli spat in the gutter.

"I feel desperate," she said.

"We were going to keep our romance a secret. Remember?"

"Nobody here cares."

She pivoted on her heels. I lingered at the window, studying the fading sky and the neon shadows up and down those water-colored streets. Marie was wrong though, somebody did care. Because then I caught sight of Chinn's undercover man in his blazer and long thin tie, up from the Mission, leaning against a corner building just beyond Zirpoli's. No doubt he'd seen me in the window kissing Marie, and I wondered how many days he'd followed me and what kind of ideas he had. Probably the cops wanted a motive for the murder. Me, acting the fool, I'd just given them a notion or two, if they didn't already have one, showing how I wanted Marie all to myself. The undercover man kept on staring. I stared back, thinking he would turn his head and scuttle away, but he didn't bother. His gaze was relentless. I pulled down the window shade and went inside, trembling.

"Marie," I said.

Marie was clearing the table, matter-of-fact, but when she turned toward me her eyes were wide. Maybe she'd heard that tremble in my voice.

"Yes, Nick."

I didn't know what to say next. She was too much for me in her blue dress. I took her by the hand and led her to the edge of the bed, meaning to talk, I think, though I'm not so sure. She pressed her lips against mine, muttering words I couldn't understand, and I rolled back onto the bed, dragging her down onto me, urging her up on top. So I made love to her that way, or perhaps it was her blue dress that I loved. I felt a hopeless enthusiasm and desire rising in my chest as I struggled to possess her, and I pulled her closer, then closer, and we grew wild for a little while, going at it until I could feel the presence of my dead brother in the room, and then I rolled Marie over so she was beneath me now and we continued more fervently than before as if to vanquish him in our delirious motion.

The next morning we lay there in the endless haze that poured through the slatted blinds. I could see the age in Marie's face but also the soft features of the girl she had been.

"What time's your appointment with Micaeli?"

"At eleven. Some kind of brunch."

"Where?"

"At his condominium. In Sausalito."

"I know that place. That's where Micaeli entertains businessmen from out of town. They take the ferry over from the city."

I wondered how she knew so much about Micaeli's affairs. Maybe I should have wondered about it longer, but she was naked on the bed beside me, vulnerable, and my mind was on other things. I watched her stand up and loop the dress over her head. She looked rumpled and delicious and sad, like somebody's wife in a television commercial, and I wanted to fuck her again.

"You still plan to meet him, don't you?"

"Sure," I said but I didn't want to go. I was afraid of what might happen out there. All my anxiety came back to me, and it seemed everything between Marie and me was a charade and we were both masking some ugly truth.

"How about if I didn't go to work for Romano?"

"What would you do instead?" Her voice was level but I knew what she was thinking. Life was expensive. I didn't make much money and wouldn't, not working for Jimmy Wong.

"It was just an idea. A wild hare."

"What are you saying?"

"We could leave. Just strike out. Not take anything from anybody." It was a bold plan, genuine action, but now it was Marie's turn to back away.

"How would we live?"

"Does it matter?"

"I don't understand," she said. "What is it you really want?"

This was my chance, I supposed. I could tell her everything I knew. But there was something hidden in her eyes and I guessed I knew what it might be and I wasn't ready yet to lose her.

"I want you," I said.

I dropped into a crouch, leaning against her, kissing the buttons on her dress. She ruffled her fingers down my neck.

"Let me iron your shirt."

Marie was not the type for ironing shirts, not usually, but we were both under the spell of that blue dress. I got the shirt for her and some clean slacks and the suit jacket Stephano's had cuffed and delivered the day before. I shined my shoes and she fussed over my clothes and we acted for a little while more like the couple in the fairy story.

"Those pictures?"

"What pictures?"

"The ones of Joe. In your photo book."

"Yes."

"The ones that are missing?"

"I don't know what you mean."

"There were some blank pages. From a few years back."

"I imagine there's a number of blank pages."

"Do you know what happened to those pictures?"

"No."

There'd always been a side to Marie that I didn't understand and that frightened me. When we were young, she'd been caught once by her uncle in Portsmouth Square, holding hands with some stranger twice her age. Rumor was that she'd had a number of affairs like that, with older men. I didn't know if I believed such stories. The talk of old women and neighborhood gossips. Marie was a wild girl, they said. Because of the father who'd disappeared. Because there was no discipline in her uncle's house. And such wildness, once it got into a girl's heart, it never went away. The first time around I'd listened to those spinsters' talk, I guess, and ended up with Anne. The second time I'd listened to my father, and ended up with nothing.

Now Marie touched the iron with her fingertips and ran it briskly across my shirt.

"You need to look good."

"Yes."

"You need to make a new start."

"I know."

"Micaeli wants to help you. Then when you're off the ground, and some time has passed, we can be a little more public. We can do things like they're supposed to be done."

"That's what I'd like to see."

She handed me the shirt and I buttoned it up. I tucked the tail into my pants and knotted my tie in the mirror.

"Then maybe you can start your own practice. We can get someplace nice. Outside the city."

"Nothing fancy."

"No. Fancy isn't important."

So the conversation went. Meanwhile I put together my wardrobe and she fussed over me, and we went on with our little theater, just the two of us, though who we were acting for and why were secrets we each kept to ourselves.

Pretty soon I was all dressed and ready to leave. If the phone hadn't rung just then, maybe everything would have been different. Maybe I would have kissed Marie good-bye, then driven over to Sausalito and Micaeli Romano and begun my new career without a hitch. Then when I got home, maybe I would've called Marie on the phone and told her all about my day. And one thing would have led to another, one working day to the next, and sooner or later I would have forgotten all about my brother's death, letting it slip away, and the police would have let it slip away too. Marie and I would have moved out of the city into one of those little cottages that people come from across the country to buy, putting down their life savings for some stucco and some wood and a bougainvillea vine outside the window. But none of that happened. Because the phone did ring and I picked it up.

It was old man Romano.

"Nick, the Hong Kong people—there's some business here, trickier than an old man like me expected. I need to talk to them alone, for the next hour, maybe a little more."

The old man's voice was all charm and sunshine. The kind of voice that makes you feel like you are standing on a hillside overlooking the sea, nothing but days ahead of you and money in your pocket.

"I understand," I said.

"I still need you here, but later. About two. This okay?"

"Yeah."

"They'll be gone then, and I can catch you up. We can talk. This is no trouble?"

"No. Not any."

"Good."

"I look forward to seeing you."

"Two o'clock."

"Sharp," I said. "With bells on my shoes."

During all this Marie stood by the slatted blinds with the light pouring all over her. The age showed more plainly in her face, and while I could still see the young Marie—her brown hair and sky-colored dress—the presence of youth and age together no longer touched me in the way it had earlier, but now each seemed to mock the other. I could see again the desperation in her eyes and the conviction that nothing would work out.

"What's going on?"

"Not much. He just changed the time. He wants me to come out a little later today."

"Why?"

"Something came up. It's just a couple hours more."

"Do you want me to stay with you?"

"No. You go home. I have some notes I should go over anyway. Legal stuff. It's good to have the extra time."

"Are you sure?"

"You go home. I'll call you when I get back."

As Marie went down the stairs, I watched her body take

on a different stride, as if escaping from under the weight that had grown between us in that room. There was a little juke to her step, like that of a young girl, and though this stirred my desire all over again, I was glad to see her go.

TWENTY-THREE
MURDER IN MY HEART

I had lied to Marie. I had no legal notes and there was nothing for me to prepare. The point of the upcoming meeting with Micaeli had not been details, rather to break me in with his Asian cronies, to do so at his waterfront condo with a big meal, a glass of wine, a handshake. The change of plans made me wonder if he'd had a change of heart. Maybe he'd talked to his son and decided to keep me in the background. Or maybe they planned to do for me like they had already done for Joe.

I went over to Mama Mia's Restaurant to grab some lunch. I tried reading the paper, just some mindless stuff, want ads and cartoons and batting averages, but my head felt empty and nothing would stick. When I looked out the window at the clouds and the sky, I felt as if they were passing through me. The people outside the window strolled through my reflection, down the pavement, and my thoughts rose up in my head, floating away before I had a chance to know what I was thinking. Then an image would bubble up: my brother's face; the apartment I'd lived in with Anne; my old law office—and I would feel anger, a knife deep in that empty head of mine, all the objects of the world etched in clarity.

I didn't like this clarity. I wanted to be rid of it. I thought a beer might help so I went down to the Naked Moon. The first show of the afternoon was a couple of hours away but Carlo, the owner, was already serving drinks. There wasn't anybody else much around, just a few crumbums and one of Carlo's girls. She had black-painted eyes and a bruise on her cheek that maybe Carlo had given her, he was that kind of guy. The place smelled of cigarettes and beer and pussy and cum, and the beer Carlo pushed me tasted as if it had been filtered through a dirty rag.

"So'd they find your brother's killer?"

"No."

"You know I saw that first wife of his down here a couple weeks back. The blonde. It was just before he died."

"Probably she was walking home. She lives up the hill."

"Maybe. But I saw her through the window, just standing there, by the meter. Then she walked on."

"And so?"

"I don't know. Nothing. I'm just saying I saw her. She ain't bad."

"How would you know?"

Carlo shrugged, sheepish. I usually got along with him well enough, though at the moment I couldn't much stand the guy. Some ways he was everything about North Beach I despised. Thick through the chest. Big arms. An accent that sounded like the stupid side of New York. He liked to tell stories about the heyday of the neighborhood, though in fact he'd only lived here a few years himself. I finished off the beer, then ordered another, drinking with my back to the bar, my stool swiveled so I could see out to the street.

"What the cops tell you about the investigation?"

"I don't want to talk about it," I said. "Give me another beer."

"You hear Gino's has reopened?"

"Gino's?"

"Yeah, you know. Gino's. In the fifties Italians came from all over to drink at Gino's. From Chicago. New York. Cleveland. Even Sinatra, the big somebody, he stopped in for a beer one time."

"I thought Gino Solano was dead."

"This is his son. Looks just like 'im."

"Must be an ugly son of a bitch."

Carlo laughed, like this was the funniest thing he'd heard in years.

"How about that beer, will you?"

He pushed it over to me. I drank it, then I ordered another.

"It's the beginning of a renaissance, you ask me," Carlo said. "The Italians are coming back."

"I'm convinced of it. Da Vinci, Pulcinella, they're all flying in tomorrow."

I remembered Gino's kid, not exactly a young man himself, maybe a dozen years older than me. I remembered him all dressed up, working the door at his father's place. We'd been on a first-name basis once upon a time, nodding to each other in the street, but I wasn't in the mood for memories. I wanted rid of that clear feeling in my head and I didn't want to be bothered thinking about Gino or Carlo or anyone else. Only now the clear feeling was being replaced with something muddy, and I thought again of those empty spaces in Marie's scrapbook. I started to got lost there in the muddiness.

Romano had arranged my brother's death. I was convinced, I told myself. Even so, there was something obvious I was missing, something right in front of me, but I still couldn't see it.

I sipped more slowly now and Carlo left me alone, realizing at last I didn't want to talk to him. He had seen me in such moods before and knew how angry a drunk can be. So he went to the other end of the bar to talk to the woman with the bruised face. Pretty soon it was one o'clock. I knew I should get going if I wanted to make my appointment with Romano, but I took my time and when I was done I slapped down a quarter for a tip, because Carlo was an ugly son of a bitch and a guy like him needed all the sympathy he could get.

I lingered outside a moment, standing in the spot where Carlo said he'd seen Marie. Though I supposed it was possible she might walk this way, coming home from downtown, maybe, it didn't seem likely, and either way I couldn't see how it mattered. A few steps further on I passed J. Ferrari's. I wouldn't have noticed the place if the door hadn't been pushed open, but it was, and I happened to glance in, and my eyes caught those of the monkey-faced little man, looking up from his sheaf of papers. There was nothing much in that office but the little man and his desk. The walls were painted black throughout, so you could not be sure the room was as small as it seemed, and there was at least the illusion of a corridor receding into the blackness behind the desk. I saw all this in an instant, and there was the slightest hesitation in my step, as if I were considering going in, and the monkey-faced little man noticed this too, as if he had seen other people make the same little hesitation. Then that moment was over, and I kept on going.

I went back up to my apartment to straighten myself up. I checked myself in the mirror, my tie was askew, and I sat at the edge of the bed telling myself I shouldn't go, I should just fuck it all off. I thought about Romano and his adopted bastard son and my brother bleeding his guts out on Linda Street. I should just walk away from them all and from Marie too, if that's what it took. I began to wish Romano had not called this morning and given me this extra time to think things over. To think about last night and about what a louse I was for screwing my brother's wife. Because if Micaeli hadn't called, I'd be out there with him already. Charmed by him like everybody was charmed. Not believing him capable of any evil in the world. But instead he'd given me these extra hours. So I kept thinking about those empty pages in Marie's book and those men's shoes in her closet. Then I did what probably had been in my mind all along. I reached into the bottom drawer. I pulled out my brother's gun. I hefted it in my hand, feeling its weight, and shoved it in my suit coat pocket. Then I drove across that beautiful bridge to the other side of the bay.

TWENTY-FOUR
THROUGH THE GATE

I drove across the Golden Gate. It's a suspension bridge, trembling and vibrating, swaying in the wind, and the combined weight of the cars rushing over sets it to trembling yet more. I remember feeling that trembling through the soles of my shoes back when I was a kid, when Joe and I would walk across on the sidewalk, cars rushing by on one side, the wind on the other, and the ocean down below. We liked to stop halfway, where the jumpers stopped, peering towards Alcatraz. We would feel ourselves suspended there, way up high, where the bay meets the ocean and the sky turns to fog, and we'd listen to the wires humming overhead with the combined trembling of all those people crossing.

Now I headed across in the center lane of traffic. I took the Sausalito exit and found my way into town.

Sausalito is like a million California towns, an old main street lined with pepper trees, silver-haired nobodies strolling underneath, doddering over the antiques. It had been a real town once. Dry docks for the building of battleships. Women who drank all day in houseboats, waiting for their husbands to return. And when they did, those fishermen, they stunk like the bay and sold their catch on the lousy wharf. These days, though, real estate was a million bucks an acre, and tourists strolled up and down the cobbled streets, charmed out of their minds. I strolled with them, gawking up at an old mansion that had once belonged to Amadeo Giannini, the Italian banker. Now it was a hotel for the rich and on the other side of its gardens stood Romano's condominium.

I passed through the old mansion grounds, flush with bougainvillea and star jasmine and flowering yuccas and birds of paradise, all growing behind the stone setbacks, tended and perfect. An Asian couple sauntered there, distinguished, well-dressed; and an older white woman in a flowered dress—beautiful, too, in her own decrepit way—sat reading beneath an umbrella. I hurried past her down a walkway that took me to Micaeli's townhouse, fashioned in imitation of the mansion behind it, a balcony off the front, glass doors opening to the bay.

The way was open and I found Micaeli inside, behind his desk. His shoulders were sloped and he moved his lips, muttering to himself like an old man.

"Nick, so good to see you!"

His face brightened as he stood up to greet me, animated now like the Micaeli he had always been, full of energy and light. The perfect Italian father. He put his arms around me, and I felt his old brown-skinned cheek against mine, and he held my shoulders between his hands and looked me in the face. I knew I had to act before my will broke down in the face of his fatherliness and his warm-hearted smile. I took a step back while he still regarded me in that way. I fumbled in my suit coat and pulled out the gun, pointing it at his heart. His smile turned to puzzlement.

"My brother, you had him killed."

"That's not true."

He walked away. It unnerved me, him turning his back on me like that, as if he did not take seriously the idea I might shoot him. I had not come to kill him, I told myself. Only to find out the truth. Micaeli, though, he simply strolled away, and this set me off. The one thing I did not want was to be taken lightly.

"Turn around. And keep your hands in front of you."

My voice, though calm and level, had a bit of the lunatic in it. Enough to get his attention. "You're the one with the gun," he said. "You don't have anything to fear from me."

"Maybe that's what Joe thought too."

"Where do you get this kind of idea?"

"It doesn't take a genius."

Micaeli eased back into his chair and his hands fell below his waist. I panicked, jutting about with the gun, and he raised them again and lay his palms flat on the desk. His manner suggested he was humoring me but I noticed also a trembling in the way he moved.

"You can kill me if you want, it's no great concern to me. I'm a dying man anyway."

"I've heard that news."

"Who told you?"

"Marie."

"She wasn't supposed to say anything, but I forgive her. The girl has no one to talk to."

"You're so considerate, Micaeli."

I said it in a wise kind of way but Micaeli, full of himself as always, did not seem to get the picture. He shrugged away his magnanimity.

"It doesn't matter. The cancer, it's in my blood now. There's no stopping it. But you—why do you ruin yourself like this? How am I going to give you a job, if this is the way you act?"

"My brother was killed by an assassin."

"Assassins kill important men. Your brother was not so important."

"The police found the man who did it. He had pictures of his victims and a picture of Joe. They were all people he killed for hire."

"I had no reason to kill your brother."

"Joe came to you a couple weeks back, didn't he?"

The old man pursed his lip and chewed on this a little bit. I didn't know how much to believe of what he might tell me, or even if he was as ill as he claimed. He seemed to have lost weight since the last time I'd seen him, true, to be more sallow, his cheeks flushed and red. It gave him a glow, not altogether unhealthy. His eyes were brighter, his lips darker, his features more pronounced, as if he were regaining the wild, handsome looks of his youth. I've heard though that such things happen. That dying people often look more beautiful for a little while, up there at the pinnacle, before the final descent.

"The way your brother came to me, his anger, it saddened me. It wasn't what I wanted. A long time ago, your mother, I was very fond of her. I promised her I would help you boys. That's why I was glad when you came to Pescadore. Who wants to leave the world with someone hating him? Because what are you, when you are gone, but what other people believe you to have been?"

I didn't want to listen to this kind of stuff. He was playing the role I'd seen him play all his life. The good patriarch. Father of North Beach. Lover of women and children. Not a perfect man, no, but kind in the heart. A man, faced with difficult decisions, who'd done the best he could. As he spoke, he made big gestures with his hands. I cut him off.

"What did you and my brother talk about?"

Micaeli looked at the gun. He was suddenly blunt. "The China Basin job. He wanted me to award him the contract."

"What did you tell him?"

"That it wasn't so easy. The city, the banks, they have their requirements. I told him I would do what I could do. But I am an old man, and no one pays much attention to me. Put the gun down, Nick. I know you're upset, but this . . . ."

"Joe had been talking to Johnny Bruno. And Bruno told him about that man you had killed."

"Johnny Bruno's an idiot."

I agreed but it didn't stop me from rabbling on, telling the whole story Johnny Bruno had told me. The story of Pavrotti's assassination that I'd heard and rejected but was now ready to believe. It did not matter for the moment that I did not have all the evidence I needed to prove Micaeli's involvement. Why should it matter? Shame was shame, pride was pride, money, money. If my brother had lived to dredge up the old story, Romano and his son might have lost the China Basin contract. But not only that. With the public attention, the old judge would have lost his dignity in his dying day, and his dignity was what he loved most.

"No." Romano scoffed and made a little dismissive notion with his hand. "It has already been dragged around, that story. When I was judge, they tried to attack me with it then. The Mussolini business. And that dead fascist in Reno. But nobody believed."

He raised his head now, taking the posture of a judge. There was something in that posture, in his voice, it would be an insult to challenge and the insult would not be to him but to yourself. I could see why the Tenney Committee had believed him and why, now, I almost believed him too. It was his manner. He had in his face the dignity of the Italian peasant, though in fact he was not a peasant, and you could hear in his voice and see in the turn of his hand a flourish that somehow stung you to the quick of your heart, making you want to weep for all those who had come to America and felt shame over who they were, and you forgave them, those Italians, their Black Shirts and their Il Duce, because they were after all only Italians, and their sons had died, and their daughters had wept, and they had given themselves in the war.

I hesitated. I lowered my brother's gun, pointing it at the floor. I remembered how everyone in North Beach had always admired Micaeli. My mother among them, myself too, looking up at him with a gleam in my eye. In the end, though, he was like all those old Italian men who wanted your admiration. When you gave it to them, they gave you a little pat on the head but nothing else in return.

"No," I said, mustering myself. "You're lying to me,"

"Why would I lie?"

"My brother went to Reno before he died. He was looking for a man named Bill Ciprione. You remember Billy, don't you?"

Micaeli said nothing.

"Oh, that's right," I said, playing it up, "you knew him as Dios. Billy Dios. An old *compagno, si*. A man who did you a favor. I'm sure, of course, you paid him well."

Micaeli kept his tongue in his head. The whites of his eyes looked yellow to me, the color of a dirty sheet on a dirty bed in a prison with walls that reached to the moon.

"Only Dios was dead," I said. "So Joe searched out the daughter. And Joe and Dios's daughter, they had a conversation."

Micaeli looked at me hard in the eye, and I looked him back. I thought of Ellen Ciprione, up there on her porch, and how'd she glanced back over her shoulder as I sat in the car, studying her. Micaeli made a little nod, and the yellow in his eyes seemed to brighten.

"You had Pavrotti killed. You paid Dios to make the arrangements."

Romano shrugged, but he didn't deny it. "The authorities sent Dios away during the war," Micaeli said.

"Afterwards, he came back, here to North Beach. He started a family—but it didn't work out for him. Myself, because of my position in the community, I felt some responsibility. I put some money for the daughter—in a blind trust. I never intended for her to find out where the money came from."

"But she did find out?"

"Dios was estranged from his family. It wasn't until a few years ago—after his first wife was dead, his brother too—that he made contact with his daughter. He wrote her a letter. And in that letter, he confessed his sins."

"The killing of Luci Pavrotti?" I asked.

He avoided the question. "The daughter came to me," he said, "the letter in her hand. On the verandah of my porch in Pescadore."

Romano's eyes were suddenly teary, full of sentiment. He made a sweeping gesture with his hand, as if he were standing on that porch, studying magnificent vistas. His property. The laborers. The young woman in front of him. His chest swelled out. He went on, telling his story in the curious way old Italians have, referring to people not by their names, but by their place within the family. Father. Daughter. Lover. The Forgotten One. Throughout it all, he went on gesturing, operatic, as if he stood on a balcony raised above a stage.

"I had feared an ugly scene. That the daughter, she would be full of the bitterness of her father. This girl, though, she began to weep. In my arms, there on the porch. There was no ugliness, only tenderness between us." Micaeli paused again, his eyes full of innuendo, as if there were something he wanted to be sure I understood. I didn't get it at first. "As time went on, things became more tender between us. Much more tender than you would think, between an old man such as myself, and a young woman. But then . . . ."

He broke it off here, but I saw the vanity in his eyes, and I knew then what he was trying to tell me. Even with one foot in the grave, these old Italians, they were full of themselves. They wanted you to know they were not tied to their wives' apron strings, and that young women still desired them. Don Juans, Casanovas unto their dying breaths, forever holding the mirror up to their own faces, whispering passionate good-byes.

"That letter, the one Dios wrote his daughter?" I asked. "My brother found out about it, didn't he?" It was a guess, but I knew suddenly it was the right guess. Joe must have had something concrete against Micaeli, or none of this made any sense. "The daughter, she told him."

"He bullied that letter out of her," Micaeli said. His voice was fierce. "She did not intend to give it to your brother. He took it."

I was still missing something though, something terrible and obvious, and maybe I was just not letting myself see. Meanwhile, Micaeli held his head in the old way, regal, full of confidence. In that moment he looked as he used to look, not so long ago really, the older man with the young man still in his eyes. He had about him the look of success, of wisdom, but of a certain charm too, one of those people whose presence is like a steep precipice, where age and youth and beauty all exist together in a single facade, and that intermingling is, in some way, irresistible. I pictured him then, standing on the verandah in Pescadore, and for a moment I could almost imagine it, the embrace, the tenderness between the young woman and the old man who had been her secret provider. I could see that embrace, maybe, the sweetness of it, and the ugliness of it too, and I could see my brother bullying that letter. There was still something wrong though. I could not picture Ellen Ciprione on that porch. Another woman, maybe, but not her.

"I didn't kill your brother," he said.

"Maybe you didn't pull the trigger—but you had it arranged."

"No. I don't know why you say that. I gave him his money, that boy. I promised him I would talk to some people. To see if he could run a crew at China Basin. I give him everything he wanted."

"Why should I believe you?"

"Your brother gave me the letter. I gave him the money he wanted. He was satisfied. I was satisfied. I had no reason to do him any harm."

"Where is this letter?"

"In my case."

"Your valise?" I asked. My heart started to beat harder now, thudding like a machine.

"Yes."

"Get it."

I wanted to see that valise, to touch it, to feel it in my hands, to know if it was the same black leather case, with the same gold zipper, that I had delivered for Jimmy Wong. Because if it was, it would prove to me what I'd already guessed. That Romano had decided to get rid of my brother—and that he used me to do it.

"It's right here. On the mantle."

He turned and picked it up and when he laid it down on the desk for me to see, all the blood seemed to rush up to my head at once, scattering my thoughts so they disappeared like flies into a damp cavern.

It was not the same valise.

Not even close. Brown leather. Old and battered. Held shut with a buckle at either end.

"I've had this for ages. It's as old as me." He fumbled with the buckles. "And opens about as easy."

"That's your case?"

"Yes."

"I have a question."

"Shoot," he said, then laughed, overhard, like this was a tremendous joke. My finger itched.

"A black valise, Italian leather. I saw it up in your office in Pescadore?"

"Oh, that."

"Who does it belong to?"

"Marie."

He smiled again, shrugging. A shadow crossed his face, as if he realized the significance of what he'd just told me, how it tied Marie to my brother's murder. Then the shadow passed and it occurred to me that perhaps he was setting Marie up the same way he'd set me. He wanted me to think she was the one who'd sent the valise to Jimmy Wong, with the money inside, to pass along to the killer.

"How did it get to Pescadore?"

"After your brother died, she came to visit. The two of you came together. Remember? One morning, she and I, we talked a while in my office—before you went down to the beach. She left the case behind. You know women, so forgetful."

He paused, as if having second thoughts, and looked at me with concern. "You should forget all this. Your brother was hell-bent for destroying himself—but you need not do the same. There is no reason to get all tangled up in the past."

"It's too late now."

"Just turn away and go. You can have your job. We'll pretend this didn't happen. I'll be dead in a few months, and none of this will matter. There's no sense in embarrassing everyone in the community."

"It's not the community I'm worried about."

"Marie's in my will. I know about the two of you. You have my blessings. She's a young woman after all, and there's no reason for me to be jealous."

"Jealous?"

It did not make sense to me. He's losing his composure, I thought, babbling. What cause did I have to be jealous of him? Then I saw the vanity in his face again, the bit of smugness. I felt a spear of panic in my heart, and there was a wave of blackness, a moment of not seeing.

"Give me the letter," I said.

Micaeli sensed the change in me, as if he had said something he shouldn't. He struggled with the buckles, grunting and wheezing. He was nervous now, looking at the gun in my hand, and I wondered if he had the letter with him at all, or if he were stalling, and this was some kind of ruse. He hurried, as if reading my mind and knowing I didn't believe him, and when he reached inside the bag, he paused a moment, and there was that look, those soft eyes, the fatherly smile on the old brown face, and as he fixed me with those eyes, a gun, I thought, he's reaching for a gun, and I was torn, not knowing what to do, or whether to believe anything he had told me.

"Don't move," I said but he didn't listen. He moved anyway. Or I thought he moved. I pulled the trigger and shot him through the heart. He went on looking at me, with that wide open expression, blood started to come up out of his mouth, an infinity of time passed, in which it seemed he would never die, and so I pulled the trigger a second time. His body made a wild jerk and he was dead.

I rummaged around in the case. There was no gun. Only the letter he had mentioned. I put it my pocket. Then I glanced down and saw his shoes.

They were the same shoes I had seen in Marie's closet.

Then I realized the truth. It had not been Ellen Ciprione on that porch with Micaeli. Of course not. Ellen Ciprione was not the old man's type. And I remembered something else. Billy Dios had two daughters. The daughter I wanted to talk to—the one who had come to Romano with her father's letter in her hand—that daughter was not Ellen Ciprione. No, she was a different woman altogether, and that woman lived much closer to home.

I had known it all along, I told myself. Or I should have known.

TWENTY-FIVE
INTERLUDE

I left the way I had come, through Giannini's garden. The old woman in the flowered dress sat as before, under her umbrella, still absorbed in her book. The Asian couple had sauntered off and there was no one else to recognize me. On Main Street I tried to control my gait, slowing down, more casual. It did not matter though because no one paid me any mind. At the last corner a young woman smiled and I smiled back. That was all the attention I got. In my car I fumbled for a while, searching for my shades on the dash, dropping my keys, until finally I hit my rhythm and disappeared from Sausalito, anonymous behind the wheel.

It was a beautiful day, the kind in picture books. As I sped over the bridge, the high pylons towering in front of me, the cables looping in the rearview mirror behind, the air seemed scented with possibility and I felt a delirious calm of the sort I've only read about in books, experienced by ascetics and priests. I had a fleeting thought I should get rid of the gun somewhere on the Marin headlands. Stand on a cliff, hurl it in the water. I didn't do it though; I didn't want to call attention to myself. It would be easier in the city. Then I could simply wipe the gun clean, drop it down an iron grate, into the sewers of Chinatown. When that was done, despite everything, Marie and I could escape all that had happened and make our way into the future.

That unexplainable feeling of clear-eyed well-being, of relief and calm, stayed with me until I was over the bridge and into the city. It disappeared as I drove down Bay Street into North Beach. My chest tightened. I thought of the Asian couple in the courtyard. I thought of the old woman with her book. I thought of the young woman who had smiled at me on the corner and even the toll-taker at the bridge. Any of them might identify me. And there were others too who knew I had gone to visit Micaeli that afternoon. Romano's son. His wife. Probably my name was even written inside his appointment book, alongside his business buddies from Hong Kong.

I found a parking place on Broadway, and pulled out the envelope, and when I glanced at it, my heart began to race all over again. The letter had been mailed from Billy Ciprione at the Alta Hotel. It was addressed, of course, to Marie Donnatelli.

Billy Dios was Marie's father. No war hero, dead in Korea. Rather he was one of those petit fascists, as they called them, men exiled during World War Two.

The letter told Dios's story. How he'd come back to North Beach after the war, tried to start a little family, but the old ghosts haunted him. Everything like Micaeli had said, only with names provided now, places. The woman Dios had abandoned was Marie's mother, six months pregnant. Then there was the part Micaeli wouldn't talk about. "In my younger days, when I first come to Reno," Dios wrote, "I did some things maybe a man shouldn't do." One of those things had been to arrange the murder of Pavrotti. He'd done it at the request of Micaeli Romano. It was a horrible thing to do, maybe, Dios admitted, but then Pavrotti was a horrible man. The fascists had turned out to be rotten, stupid to the core, betraying everyone, and that stupidity had ruined his life. So he'd been happy to help out his old friend Micaeli, who in turn helped out Dios's estranged family in North Beach.

After Pavrotti's death, wrote Dios, he went straight. He went into the foundation business, started a new family, always with his old family in mind. He told his story quickly and simply. As the letter approached its end, the handwriting grew more slanted and crude, barely legible.

Now, my first wife, your mother, she is dead. My second wife too, and it will not be too long before I follow. But I want my daughter in North Beach to know her father did not forget her. He thought of her all these years. She was his little girl, and it broke his heart, everything, the way it happened. Now he wants nothing more than her forgiveness.

Forgive me, please.
Your father,

Billy Dios

The letter had been postmarked several years back. It had taken Billy Dios a while to die, in his little room in the Alta Hotel. Whether he'd gotten his forgiveness or not, though, that was something I didn't know.

I put the envelope back into my pocket and got out of the car. In the afterglow of the shooting, so close to the death, I had felt as if anything could be accomplished. I had liberated myself, Marie, all of us. Now, standing on the corner of Columbus and Grant, looking down into the giant maw of the past, that street where all the old Italians had strolled and strutted and fought their battles with one another over who were the real Italians, it seemed escape was impossible. I put one foot in front of the other and hurried my way up those concrete stairs toward Marie's apartment on Telegraph Hill.

TWENTY-SIX
THE FINAL CHAPTER

I thumbed the buzzer six times before she answered, three quick bursts, then three more, with no patience inbetween. Her hair was damp and she looked unraveled in the heart and pale in the face, disturbed at the sight of me. I still had the revolver in my pocket and my sunglasses on. The lenses were cheap, the inside of the apartment dark as steel.

"Did you talk to Micaeli?"

"Yes."

"I didn't expect to see you so soon."

"It wasn't a long conversation."

We stood in the kitchen now. She was looking at my chest, at my shirt, and I looked too and noticed a dark stain. I touched the stain with my finger and it came away damp. I could not tell the color of the stain but then I lifted the glasses and saw it was blood. Before leaving I had rolled Romano over to take the money out of his wallet, to make the whole thing look like a burglary. His blood had been everywhere and now it was on my shirt.

I took out the letter from her father and placed it on the counter between us. Marie glanced at the envelope, recognizing it. Then her lips turned in the slightest smile, the kind you get when you know everything has gone wrong and in ways you never anticipated.

"You changed your clothes. That's an Italian sweater, isn't it? Cashmere. Expensive stuff." I strolled up and touched the fabric, standing close. Her stomach was warm and I could feel her breathing underneath. "Or did you get it on sale?"

"What are you trying to say?"

"Just admiring."

"The dress was dirty," she said. "Maybe you should change too. That shirt—I've got something in my closet." She looked at my shirt more closely. "Are you bleeding?"

"No, sweetie. And watch what you get from the closet. If it belonged to the old man, it won't fit."

"That was three years ago, Nick," she said. She admit-

159

ted it quickly, not bothering to argue, like sleeping with the old man was a small thing, it didn't really matter. She turned away from me though, avoiding the darkness I knew was in my eyes. "It didn't last but a few months," she said. "Only a little recharge now and then. Right? Paid for your apartment, didn't he? Put you in his will?"

"What happened over there?"

"Everyone thought it was his son you were fucking."

"Stop it," she said. "You sound like your brother."

"Joe found out about your father in Reno. About the letter. He knew everything."

"Joe was blackmailing Micaeli. I wanted to tell you, but I didn't know how."

"So you arranged to have him killed?" I asked. "Was that Micaeli's idea? Or yours?"

Her head jerked a little when I said that, like maybe she'd been slapped, and she walked over to the window, looking at those stairs that wound down to the ravine. Then the clarity was back all of a sudden, white-knuckled, bright as hell. Marie stood in the middle of that clarity, and I felt for a minute as if all the electricity in the city were charging through my heart.

"Micaeli didn't have anything to do with it," she said, and looked up from the ravine.

Suddenly I didn't want her to talk anymore. I wanted to run over and put my hand over her mouth and tell her to be quiet. I wanted to shake her hard until the words in her mouth broke apart and there wasn't anything left for me to hear. But I'd already started her going, and it was too late now.

"Your brother was never going to let me be" she said.

"You should've locked the door."

"I tried that when we were married. It didn't work. Then, a few weeks ago, he came over here again." She glanced down at the envelope again, and I glanced, too, and remembered how when we were kids, all those stories she'd told about her father, the war hero, the adventurer, the man who roamed the world. She shivered, shaking hard, like she needed comfort, but I couldn't go to her now.

"Joe knew my real name was Dios. It was on my marriage license. He didn't know about my father, though. I only found out myself a few years ago. About the time of the divorce."

"You kept it a secret?"

"I visited my father once, only once. His other daughter was there, Ellen, from the other marriage—and I guess I just didn't like the whole thing. I didn't want to know them, I didn't want to know the things he had done, or to have other people know. So that was the end of it. There was nothing else between us after that. Except—I did hold onto his letter."

"What happened?"

"A few weeks ago, Joe came across my father's name in a death notice. He recognized it and he talked to Johnny Bruno and he put things together. He talked to me first, but I wouldn't say anything, so he went to Reno and sweet-talked Ellen Ciprione. He got her drunk, and she told him everything—and she told him all about the letter too.

"Then Joe came back, looking for the letter. I told him no, he couldn't have it. We had a fight, a big one. Loud. Noisy. He gave me a push, and he kicked me; he all but knocked me cold on the stairs. Then he locked the door—and by the time I got in, he'd torn the place apart."

I didn't say anything. I was thinking about the bruise on her thigh, and the fight the neighbors had overheard. And I was imagining my brother, masquerading himself to Ellen Ciprione, drinking with her in some casino, hustling her, maybe even sleeping with her, leaving her to wake up alone in that harsh desert light. No wonder, when I showed up a few weeks later, she was suspicious. Another man, a cop, a thug, insurance agent, it didn't matter, each one a brother to the other, full of the same crap. So she'd sent me packing.

"I realized he was never going to stop, " Marie said, "he was always going to be here banging on my door. And now—he was after Micaeli too."

"I thought Micaeli paid him off."

She laughed. "Joe had a copy of the letter. He wasn't going to let anyone off so easy."

"So Micaeli had him killed?"

161

"I told you—Micaeli didn't have anything to do with it."

I knew what she was saying, but I didn't want to believe her. I wanted to think it was the old man's doing. "You did it for Micaeli's money," I said. "To keep it coming your way."

"No" she said. Her voice was angry. "I did it to get your goddamn brother out of my life. Or that was part of it. Then, at the funeral, I saw you. And I realized something else."

I sighed deep, then put my hand in my pocket and felt the gun. I remembered Micaeli and the awful look on the dead man's face as I knelt over him, rummaging his pockets.

"How did you arrange it?"

"J. Ferrari's."

And she didn't have to say anything else, because I could picture the rest. Marie walking inside that pitch-dark room, handing over to that ugly little man her valise, the money, the pictures for the assassin. Then that monkey-faced bastard had passed it through another pair of hands into Chinatown. Of course he wouldn't have handled it himself. What route that package then took to Jimmy Wong's desk, I didn't know and probably never would. Maybe Wong handled such things continually, or maybe he owed J. Ferrari a favor, but either way that valise had made its way over into Chinatown, moving down those alleyways where desire attaches itself to every coincidence, so that Wong handed the valise to me, not knowing, maybe, that he delivered into my hands the instrument of my brother's death.

I pulled Joe's gun out of my pocket now and brandished it in a broad, stupid way, so Marie could see. "This was Joe's. I found it in his house, in that old jacket he used to wear."

"You took that to Micaeli's?"

"I killed him."

"You son of a bitch," she said. Her eyes were filmy and she put her head in her hands. "We could have been together. You and me. Now you've ruined everything."

I felt the distance rolling in between us now, like fog on a dense and forgotten street, and the longer we stood there the further apart we seemed, until everything in the last few weeks seemed to have happened on some shrouded corner in a city I would never see again. I wanted to lose myself in that fog.

"You were blackmailing the old man," I said. "Blackmailing him and fucking him. To keep the money rolling in. You even got yourself into his will."

Maybe it was true, or maybe her feelings toward the old man were sincere, but either way it was a son-of-a-bitch thing to say. Marie turned her head, one hand on her cheek, hurt, maybe, resigned, as if I had touched some naked place no one was supposed to touch. I regretted my words, almost. Marie closed her eyes, her mouth was parted, her face flushed, and she seemed to be studying something in the darkness inside, as a child might, then she opened her eyes. She looked as if she wanted to tell me something, only there were no words for the thing she wanted to say. In that instant she seemed—I don't know the words either—she seemed suddenly luminous and innocent but sluttish too, as if the innocence and its corruption were all mixed together, and she had brought them out of the dark. I imagined then how things had really been between Romano and her. The old man, the younger woman. The moment between them on the porch. The need to protect and be protected, tender, almost fraternal (I didn't see lust, I told myself, I didn't see lust) and then my brother threatened to batter all that down. To expose her father and ruin Micaeli. In the end, Marie had acted to protect Romano—and to protect herself, of course—and she'd acted in the same manner her father had acted so many years before. Then she and I had seen each other across Washington Square, that day in the fog, and before long Joe was in the ground, and we were in each other's arms, where we'd both wanted to be all along. It was me that she loved.

That's what she wanted to tell me, more or less (or so I tell myself now, here in this prison); that's what I saw in her eyes as she turned to speak. Then the moment passed and I saw it the other way. She had murdered my brother. She

163

and the old man. And they had tried to put it on me.

"I can't go to jail," she said. "I can't live, not like that."

She arched away from me and I watched her as I'd watched so many times before, how her body moved beneath her clothes, her cashmere pullover, her black skirt, as she pushed up close to the sliding door and peered out over the houses to the blue water of the bay. "There's no going back once it's over. I should've known that. Everything's finished."

"We could run," I said. "The two of us, we could get out of town before they find Micaeli's body."

She didn't say a word but she didn't need too, because we both knew this would never work. We could never get away. We didn't have any plans, and she'd given all her money to Ferrari, and if we ran they would find us sooner or later, in a motel in Tucson or San Diego or some damned place, and our hair would be dyed and I would have on a cheap suit and maybe seventy dollars I'd heisted from a liquor store along with the vague notion of escaping over the border. If we stayed here in North Beach, I'd be in jail before the day was out and Marie would end up in the women's prison across the bay for arranging my brother's death. So the best it could be for us now was long gray days and romantic little notes on prison stationery. Marie let out a moan, thinking these same thoughts maybe, and I had the urge to comfort her, to touch her, to tell her I would lie to Chinn so she could stay free. Instead, I thought of her in Romano's arms and of my brother lying dead and I glanced down at the gun in my hand. The anger rose in my heart.

"Go ahead," she said, like she was reading my mind. "Everything's over."

She didn't mean it, maybe, like people never mean such things, and in a moment or so, her courage would've faded. Still, she arched her spine, waiting. And when I saw the soft hollow of her back, revealed there beneath the cashmere, I desired her more than before and hated her more too. I pointed the gun at her back and she just stood there straight as a corpse. I only wanted her to say something, to hear again how she'd loved me all along and risked everything for me, it was all for me. I wanted to capture that moment again. A fog horn called out in the bay, a melancholy noise. No, I thought, it's all a lie. She set me up. Then she moved, turning her head just a little.

"Nick," she said.

I heard the plaintiveness in her voice, the desire, all the things I wanted to hear, and when I heard them I felt a tug at my heart and I pulled the trigger.

She lurched forward into the glass, her face flat into it and her hands raised, palms against the window. She slid slowly and as she did blood blossomed at the back of her cashmere sweater, then she tumbled the rest of the way, all at once, crumpling at the knees, twisting as she fell. She ended on her back, one hand flung out dramatically and her eyes still open. She was looking at me. I was looking back. I could see inside her to that dark place suddenly full of light. Then something changed in her eyes and I knew she was dead. The blood came through the front of her sweater now. There was a bullet hole in the sliding door.

(Marie told me once that I had no nerve. That I let myself be carried away in the moment, but could not take action of my own. Even so, I pulled the trigger. I did it because I loved her, I tell myself now, to save her from jail. To keep for myself that moment when I had seen how she was, and how things might have been. Because if she lived I knew what would happen. How they would sequester us, then turn us against one another in court. How—to save herself—she would say that I was the one who had planned it all. Her attorney would point at me. Jack-n-ape, he would say, jealous bastard. Murderer. And the jury would look at me, and Marie's face would go slack, as if she believed it herself, and I would have no choice but to pull her down too. We would be at each other's throats, a charming spectacle. I didn't want to be part of that. So I pulled the trigger. That's what I tell myself. Though when I go back to that moment and remember and look down, it isn't my own hand pulling the trigger but someone else's, a moment out of another man's life.)

I stumbled from the apartment. I was almost to the bottom of Filbert Street before I realized I still held the gun in my hand. An old woman was coming around the corner and

I got rid of it as fast as I could, wiping the prints in a half-ass way and tossing it in the bushes.

As I walked, I felt none of that elation I'd felt driving across the bridge, only a dumb awareness that fate had worked itself out and was in some way satisfied. I was dead calm, my head empty. Maybe someplace inside I thought ahead to the court case and the stories that would appear in the papers. How in the end it would read like one of those stories you hear happening in these little corners of town, where the people have known each other too long and lived too close together. Maybe that's what I was thinking. Or maybe I was thinking ahead to how they would put me here in this gray room, on an endless series of appeals, with another gray room waiting down the hall, and another beyond that, while meanwhile I dreamed about a day that would never come, when I would be released and walk the long hills on my way to a little bungalow where my true life would begin. Or maybe none of this was what I thought, and I was simply walking down the street, wondering what I would do when this calm left me, as surely it would, and I would have no choice but to fight the shaking inside.

I know, as I turned toward the wharf, onto lower Columbus, I had no notion of escape. I only wanted a drink, that was all, and there was Gino's place on the corner up ahead.

It was small place, built in the '50s, a cottage cheese ceiling overhead and a space-prow for a bar, and behind that bar there was Gino mixing drinks. A Chinese couple sat in the far back, a pair of fags closer up, a beatnik at the counter. Gino was in his fifties somewhere and he did resemble his father. He had his hair shoe-blacked and a big handlebar mustache and a sign on the counter that read:

God is an Italian.

I pointed at the sign. I gestured largely, like a man on stage, and spoke too loud. "Tell God to give me a drink. A scotch. With plenty of ice, and no water."

Gino got out his bottle and poured. He slid the drink across the counter.

"God sends you his blessings," he said. "Where you been keeping yourself, Nick?"

"In the neighborhood."

I took the drink down fast. I could feel Gino's eyes sliding over me but if he noticed the blood stain on my shirt, it didn't mean anything to him, at least not yet. I felt like weeping.

"Another one."

"Sure, sure," he said and poured it up for me. Then the phone started ringing in a little room just behind the bar. There was no door on that room, and Gino answered the phone in that accent he'd inherited from his father, loud and bursting with its own importance; then all of a sudden he dropped his voice and turned his back on me. The hunch in his shoulders deepened. In a little while he hung up and dialed another number on his own.

When he returned, he tended to me quick, pouring another drink. His eyes passed over me again. Remembering the stain, I glanced down at myself, then back at Gino, and in that glance it passed between us what had happened on the phone. (I didn't realize then, of course, exactly how it had happened. I couldn't know that the old woman on the street had seen me throw down the gun: that she'd followed me at a distance and watched me go into Gino's. An Italian woman, of course. Now she would have another story to tell the old ones out on the bench in Washington Square. A story to tell in between those others they told over and over. This one about that nobody eviction agent. How she'd tracked me down. Called Gino from the phone booth on the corner, warning him, and Gino had called the cops.) There was an instant of fear in Gino's eyes now, maybe he'd sensed my suspicion, but then that was gone. His eyes passed over me once more, and he nodded, and I nodded too. He gave me a look like I was a *paesano*, like we were brothers in this blood. Then he moved away.

I was alone at the counter.

I swiveled on my stool, looking through the thick blue light at the patrons in Gino's bar: the Chinese couple up from the suburbs, so demure and sweet, the gays whispering into one another's ears, the poet scribbling in his endless little book. Meanwhile a Mexican girl washed dishes in the back, and Gino stepped out of sight somewhere behind her. I finished my drink and heard a siren nearby. The station wasn't far. I could've run, I guess, but there was nowhere for me to go and my gun was back in the bushes. "One more," I yelled out to Gino, and I lit a cigarette. Gino didn't come. I put the cigarette to my lips. I inhaled its dark smoke, and all the smoke in that bar, it seemed. This was the moment I had been moving towards all along.

There was another siren now, closer. Any minute the cops would be at the end of the block, turning the corner. I could imagine them already, climbing from their squad cars, hurrying down the sidewalk, Leonora Chinn out in front, of course, moving crisply, her head held so straight and true. She would be the first one through the door, pausing under the picture of Il Duce. I wondered for a minute about those other cops behind her, whether they would be men or women, and whether their skin would be brown or yellow or white as the driven snow. In this city it was impossible to say. They could be any color at all, I thought, but one thing I knew for certain, their uniforms would be midnight, the deepest shade of blue.